THE PERFECT HOME

KEVIN LYNCH

INKUBATOR
BOOKS

Published by Inkubator Books
www.inkubatorbooks.com

Copyright © 2022 by Kevin Lynch

ISBN (Paperback): 978-1-915275-08-0
ISBN (eBook): 978-1-915275-09-7
ISBN (Hardback) 978-1-915275-13-4

Kevin Lynch has asserted his right to be identified as the author of this work.

THE PERFECT HOME is a work of fiction. People, places, events, and situations are the product of the author's imagination. Any resemblance to actual persons, living or dead is entirely coincidental.

PROLOGUE

He didn't see the first blow coming, just heard a sudden swooshing sound fill the air, then a fizzing bolt of pain that flashed from his head to course through his body. His knees buckled, and he sank slowly to the floor. He reached out for something to hold and felt the softness of the long sofa where he had spent so many happy years brush against his fingertips before he slid completely to the floor. There was a loud ringing in his ears on the side of his head where he had been hit, but through that ringing, he could hear the heavy, determined breathing of his attacker. His own breathing felt suddenly weak and shallow. The trickle of air that came into his lungs gave him no energy. His muscles felt soft and useless. He lay splayed on the floor and tried, through blurred vision, to make out the shape of his attacker. He stood over him, blocking the light.

He heard another swoosh and felt a second blow impact heavily against his shoulder. The force of the blow was so strong that his whole body shifted a few inches. Bolts of electric pain rushed from the shoulder. At the same time, as he tried to move his arm on that side, it felt floppy, weak and useless. He was trapped, exactly where he lay, unable to move anything, here on the floor of his living room, a place so familiar to him. Now, this was the same place where he was going to meet his end, and there was nothing he could do about it.

He tried to speak, to ask for mercy, but his voice trickled out in a thin whisper. The air had seeped almost completely from his lungs, and they felt like they were being filled with something solid and heavy. To try to breathe was an act that flooded him with searing pain. He saw the shadow of his attacker shift in the light. He was breathing heavily with the effort of the blows he was raining down.

There was a pause, and that was followed by another swooshing sound that ended with an impact to the side of his head, which sent urgent currents of electricity flowing through him, searching to ground themselves, to find a resting place, but there was nothing there. The currents travelled hopelessly through him, through what had once been an able and fit body. They could find no place to ground themselves, and he knew at that moment that they never would again.

1

I love gardening, so that evening I was out front tending to my lavender, my heather patch, my sweet pea, my jasmine, making sure all my little babies were trimmed back, deadheaded, watered, whatever needed to be done to keep them in their late spring bloom. I don't have much of a back garden, more of a yard, so all the hot action takes place out front. I live in a cul-de-sac, at the very top, centre house, so I get to see all the comings and goings on the street. Generally, it's quiet, residential, not much happening, the odd cat peering out from a driveway, people coming back from work, kids on bicycles, maybe someone knocking a football around, but quiet and settled would be how you'd describe it. Maybe I should qualify that description and say that's how you would have described it because that evening marked a change where things would never be the same again.

He drove up in a long, low-rider-style car. Its engine emitted a deep growl of untapped power as he swung into the driveway of the newly rented house two doors down from me. I was snipping a couple of dead leaves off my jasmine plant and encouraging its train through some of the higher parts of the small trestle I had fixed against my front wall. His car was a metallic purple colour, and the exhaust looked big enough to cook a pizza.

After the car pulled in, nothing happened for a good two minutes. It sat there like it was a self-driving vehicle and had come to rest in its new home, waiting for further instructions. The windows were tinted, so I could see nothing of what was going on inside. I half-expected the car to start up and wheel itself back out of the driveway, but slowly, agonizingly, the driver's door opened, and I saw first a leg with blue jeans and brightly coloured trainers, then a midriff with a steel-buckled belt, then finally, a muscular torso in a T-shirt and a solid, square-jawed head. He smiled as he stepped out and swept his gaze slowly around the estate, stopping only when he rested his eyes on me. I gave him a small wave, my snipping tool in hand, then went back to tending the plants.

In that animal, instinctive way we have, I knew he was still looking at me, and sure enough, when I half-lifted my head a minute later, he was still in exactly the same spot and looking over. I think I gave a half-wave again because I wasn't sure what else to do, and it was then he started walking towards me. There was no sense of hurry in his walk. It was more of an amble, as if he were appreciating all the sights and sounds of spring on our street, but at the same time, there was something demanding, almost menacing in his approach. It was like he had arrived to survey something that was rightfully his and expected neither complaint nor resistance as he claimed it.

I went back to tending the plants because I didn't want to watch as he strolled over. When I heard his footsteps close by, I looked up again. He looked from me to the jasmine and sniffed deeply.

'Lovely smells off those. I forget the name now.'

'Jasmine,' I said. My voice sounded hurried to me, like I

was hoping to get the encounter over with.

He cracked a wide smile that held little warmth. 'That's the one. Puts a little perfume in the air. Nothing like it.'

His voice was deep and gravelly. His eyes twinkled with a sense of restlessness when he looked at me. He swept his gaze around the rest of the garden.

'Looking good. Nice hobby. I wish I could get stuck into a pastime like that, but I'm too busy.' He held his two hands up for me to see, and they were coated with a faint shadow of black. 'Cars are my thing. You can probably tell from the motor over there.' He nodded at his low-rider. 'I fix them up and sell them on. Bit of a passion of mine. But listen, I'm forgetting my manners. Steve Murray's the name. I'm the new tenant over there. I'd shake your hand, but I still have to give myself a good scrubbing.'

'June Sweeney. Pleased to meet you.' I tried to put what sincerity I could into my voice. My motto in life is to give everyone a chance until they prove you wrong, and I'd do the same for him, although I had an uneasy feeling in the pit of my stomach and I'd only just set eyes on the man.

He stayed where he was but turned to take the street in. 'Nice, quiet place. I'm not used to living in the likes of one of these posh areas, but when I saw the place up for rent, I said to myself I had to grab this opportunity with both hands.'

'Yes, it's a quiet street with nice neighbours,' I agreed, although it had changed in recent years. When I first moved in with my now ex-husband, Nick, there were quite a few older people on the estate. Some of them had died off, and the properties were being bought up by landlords and rented. I had a college campus sitting about a hundred yards behind me, and there had been various attempts to build student accommodation right behind me, which I and my adjoining neighbour, Fred, had resisted.

'I have two little girls of my own, and it'd be nice for them to stay somewhere quiet and settled like this. Mind you, I only have them a couple of days a week. The rest of the time, they're with their ma. Things aren't exactly hunky-dory between me and her, but you don't need to know about all that.' He smiled again with that restless twinkle in his eyes.

Just then, I saw the figure of my daughter, Cathy, walking towards us. She was twenty and was in third year in college, just one more year to go. She looked every inch the college student with her satchel over her shoulder and her free-flowing mop of wavy brown hair bouncing along behind her. She was checking her phone as she walked, something I had taken issue with a number of times, as she spent so much time on it anyway, breakfast, lunch and dinner and every-thing in between. I'd asked her could she not, even for safety's sake, give the thing a rest and take in the world around her. The answer was something along the lines of she was so busy in college and really spent very little time on it compared to others, and she had to keep up with her friends, and really, what did I know anyway about the modern way of life? I choose my battles carefully with Cathy and her younger brother, Sam, so I let it slide, promising myself I'd chip away at her resistance over time on that one.

She stopped just short of us and looked up from her screen. Cathy has a clear, expressive face with hazel-coloured eyes that could exude warmth or cut you short depending on her mood. She was studying history and politics and had a strong sense of social justice. There was nothing she liked more than a good argument about the injustices of the world.

'Well, who do we have here?' Steve asked, and the comment seemed immediately intrusive.

'That's Cathy, my daughter. She's just getting back from college.'

Cathy looked at me with a touch of incredulity. 'It's okay, Mum. I can speak, you know.'

Steve smiled at that. 'We've got a live one here, I can tell.'

Normally, Cathy would launch into someone who came out with a comment like that, but she just smirked at Steve. Maybe it was the fact that he was obviously something different to what she usually encountered on our street with his tattooed arms folded over his muscular torso. Whatever it was, I wanted to hurry the meeting along.

'Your dinner is in the oven, love. Me and Sam already had ours.'

'Okay, thanks, Mam,' she said with a nonchalant swish of her hair and a final glance at Steve before she disappeared into the house. I decided I'd had enough of this encounter, so I went back to snipping the jasmine, but Steve apparently wasn't quite finished, as he stayed where he was.

'They can be trouble, but sure, you have to love them. My two girls will be just like that one of these days. They're at that innocent age now. Need a lot of minding, though. Speaking of which, I'll need a babysitter fairly regular between this and that while I'm here, and I'm guessing your Cathy could do with a little earner on the side. Life isn't getting any cheaper, that's for sure, what with the phones and everything.'

He took a last look around my garden, nodding to himself with apparent approval before ambling back to his car and opening the back door. There was a brief flurry of activity in which I could see him grabbing for something before two nasty-looking pit bulls emerged looking frantically at their new surroundings. Steve held them securely by two long chains that were attached to their collars, and he dragged them off to hustle them into a side passage that led to the back of his house. He closed the wooden gate of the side passage behind him, but I was left with the image of the two brutish faces scouring our street before they were bundled out of sight.

2

M y new neighbour played on my mind that night and on into the next day. As a social worker, I have to deal with trauma on a daily basis, and that day was no different. A young girl had to be taken from a home that had broken down due to drugs and alcohol. It was my job to find her emergency accommodation and fill in all the necessary paperwork. The parents weren't too happy about it, but the police had to be called the night before for a major disturbance in the house, and the child was taken into their care. I picked her up from the police station and set about finding her somewhere safe. I knew the system well, so I had somewhere for her within a couple of hours and spent the rest of the time doing the paperwork.

Driving into my estate later that evening, I had a sense of trepidation that I'd never had before. I believe that intuition keeps a couple of paces ahead of us in anticipating the future, so I was busy peering over at Steve's house as I pulled into my short driveway. I didn't have to look too hard to find him. His own car was out on the street, and he was in overalls under another low-rider-type car that was jacked up in his drive. I could hear the sound of metal against metal as he did whatever he was doing. In the background, I could hear the frantic snuffling and occasional barking of his dogs, which were mercifully behind the gate at the side of his house.

I walked into my own house and, to my surprise, was greeted by the aroma of freshly fried bacon. Cathy was at the cooker with clouds of steam billowing in the air around her.

'Cooking?'

I must have looked surprised because Cathy opened her arms in a 'yeah, and?' gesture.

'That's nice,' I threw in quickly to disguise the fact that it was an actual miracle that Cathy had even known where the cooking utensils were kept, never mind picked them up with any intent.

'Dad's coming over. He texted me earlier. He's in the "hood", as he likes to call it. I'm doing carbonara and garlic bread.'

'Lovely.' I tried to sound as nonchalant and easy-going as I could, but the prospect of facing my ex over dinner did nothing to raise my spirits. We had an agreement that he'd get in touch if he was going to drop by. Our separation had been acrimonious, to say the least, after I'd discovered that he'd been having an affair with my friend Ciara for a couple of years. Our agreement was nothing to do with Cathy, so I just let it slide.

I went upstairs, showered, and generally put on as convivial a face as I could before I heard the doorbell ring, followed quickly by footsteps and then the sound of Nick's voice booming around the hall.

'I see you have new neighbours,' was his first comment when I appeared.

'Neighbour, singular.'

'No.' He nodded out the window, where I could indeed see a small van being unloaded by a couple of student types.

'Oh, 'cos we got the mechanic guy in last night.' I nodded in the other direction, toward Steve's.

'And he's not bad-looking,' Cathy threw in cheerily.

Sam came down from whatever corner of the house he'd been hiding in and sat at our wooden dining table. We have a kitchen-cum-dining room, so you can see all the way up the street from the table.

'Think I recognize that guy from college,' he said, brushing his mop of curly hair up off his face to get a clearer view.

'Yep, things changing on the street. I'm not surprised with the new extension on the college. They're going to be crying out for more accommodation,' Nick said as we all sat down and watched Cathy tease heaps of steaming spaghetti onto our plates.

'I'm not having student accommodation looming over our backyard,' I said as the spaghetti slid around the plate to find its eventual resting shape.

'Hopefully not. Now, how are the students doing?' Nick asked, flicking his head from Sam to Cathy.

'Tons of assignments now that we're near the end of the year,' Cathy responded, twisting a forkful of spaghetti into a negotiable shape.

'Loads to do to keep the sports scholarship for next year,' Sam said sullenly.

'Well, getting in on a scholarship was an amazing feat. You just have to keep the soccer up and go to all the training, I guess,' Nick mused.

'Yeah, and loads of assignments about anatomy and stuff that we're never going to need to know.'

'Well, you might decide to go for physio in the end, so keep the options open.'

We drifted into a spell of silent eating that was suddenly

interrupted by the violent revving of a powerful engine. All our heads swivelled in the direction of the noise.

'My God, that's loud,' I said, craning my neck to see what Steve might be up to.

'He's really into his cars,' Nick offered.

'And we are really into our nice, quiet street.'

'Oh, come on, Mom, it's only seven in the evening. No harm in having a bit of life outside.'

'Depends what kind of life you're talking about, Cathy. That particular version I can do without.'

'Mom, you're sounding a bit snobby there. Like, that's what he's into, so who are we to judge?'

'We'll see who's judging when they're trying to get a three-thousand-word essay done with half an hour to the deadline.'

'Mom, that was only once or twice, so don't keep going on about it. It's good to have a mix of the social strata on the road. Too much homogeneity is poisonous.'

I held my counsel at that stage. Once Cathy starts throwing words like 'homogeneity' around, you know you're about to take a plunge down some academic rabbit hole.

'Yeah, maybe he'll bring a bit of colour to the street.'

'It's all very well to say that if you're not actually living on the street,' I replied to Nick but regretted it as soon as I said it, not because I didn't want to offend him but because I knew the kids didn't like reminders of the fact that we were separated.

'Dad's right,' Sam put in. 'If everyone's the same, it's just . . .' He paused as he searched for the right word, looking from left to right with what I had to admit was a kind of irritating, although simultaneously cute, frown creasing his forehead. 'It's just boring.'

For the rest of the meal, we managed to avoid any 'hot' topics except Nick mentioned that his gardening business had hit a bit of a dip, which surprised me, seeing as we were in late spring, a time when he should be pretty damn busy. I wondered if he was gently trying to tell me he'd be late with his maintenance payments for the month, but I let it slide.

However, his luck took a sudden upturn as we were all saying goodbye at the door. A fair-haired gent with a proprietorial air was watching the new students move the last of their stuff from the van, and I saw him hand over a set of keys.

He turned to see Nick walking towards his pickup, which he had emblazoned with a gardening name and logo on the side.

'Jim McCann,' the fair-haired gent said, extending a hand toward Nick. 'I'm the agent who's looking after a couple of properties on the street. I'd been meaning to introduce myself.'

'I'm the owner of the house,' I said to McCann, nodding back towards my house as if there would be any mistaking what I was talking about.

'Of course,' he replied. 'I wasn't making any assumptions . . .' He let that sentence trail off because he probably *was* making assumptions, but he regathered with admirable speed. 'It's always good to meet the residents just so we're all singing off the same hymn sheet.'

Nice ambiguous turn of phrase, I thought, although I was pretty sure we wouldn't be sharing any hymn sheets.

He marched towards me and gave me a vigorous handshake that, I have to admit, had a certain old-world charm about it. His hands were dry and warm, and there was at least the appearance of sincerity in the effort he put into it. Besides, he was easy on the eye, late forties, fair hair that was tousled over a broad, welcoming face.

'It's a wonderful street you have here.' He turned to take in the street like some Napoleonic figure surveying a happy outcome on the battlefield.

'Yes, it is, and we go to great lengths to keep it that way.'

He dropped his smile for a fraction of a second when he heard that, but he quickly regathered his bonhomie.

'Well, that's what I was going to talk to—' he gave a look at the side of the pickup where Nick had his name scrawled in bold, black lettering '—to Nick about.' He looked back to Nick, who was standing beside his pickup. 'I couldn't fail to notice you do some gardening work, and well, with an expanding portfolio of properties, my client is looking for someone who can tend the gardens. Don't mean to put you on the spot, so no need to give an answer now. Here's my card. Give me a shout anytime.'

Nick took the card and stuck it in his wallet. McCann started clambering back into his car—a silver Merc—when I spotted my neighbour Fred walking quickly down his drive towards us. He had his hand up, beckoning to McCann to stay. McCann climbed back out of his car again and proffered a hand towards Fred, who didn't accept the offer but used his free hand to point over at Steve's house.

'Do I gather that you are an estate agent or landlord, and are you responsible for that house over there?'

McCann followed his pointing finger to the drive of Steve's house, where the low-rider he was working on was at a tilt with some bricks under it.

'Yes, Mr Murray is on our books.'

'Well, I hope he doesn't intend turning this place into some sort of makeshift garage because we won't tolerate that here.'

Fred had the house that was directly beside Steve's, so he would be the one who was most impacted.

McCann looked briefly befuddled, like he wasn't used to getting complaints. 'We keep a close eye on all the tenants, but really, it's the landlord who has the last say. If you have any complaints, we'd be glad to hear them, but don't forget

Mr Murray has only just moved in. Everyone needs to be given a chance, don't you think?'

The way he put that was pretty reasonable, and I saw Fred drop the pointing hand. He was an elderly man, a widower, and he was always well-dressed. His house and front garden were kept in show-house condition. He kept the garden low maintenance with just short grass and a couple of shrubs, but it was always neat as a pin. In contrast, Steve's was already looking positively run-down and scruffy.

'I just hope he tidies up after himself, and I can hear those dogs of his snuffling at the bottom of the gate all the time. They don't seem suitable for a quiet street like this. What if they got out? They look like a restricted breed to me.'

McCann smiled and eased back into placatory mode. 'If there are any problems, please let me know, and we'll try to sort them. The last thing we want is for the neighbours to have any issue with the tenants. Is that fair enough?'

Fred nodded uncertainly, looking less than convinced.

3

_____

As I left for work the next morning, I glanced over at Steve's house and noticed that the curtains in his front room were half-open, the car in the drive was still sitting up on blocks, his own car was out on the street, and the general appearance was one of scruffiness. I'm not one to judge. I've been through my own stuff, so I know how life isn't always the ideal thing that some people try to make it out to be. The time leading up to the separation with Nick had been harrowing. I'd first discovered the affair through the most clichéd of ways. He'd left a hotel receipt in one of his trouser pockets, and it fell out as the trousers were going into the wash. I had stared at it and tried to come up with some reason for its existence but failed because Nick had never mentioned staying in a hotel. He had, however, told me he was going to visit his elderly mother in the country and wanted to go 'solo' because she would be less uptight, and he felt like they needed a heart-to-heart.

When I confronted him, he'd started making all sorts of excuses about needing some space when he was with his mum and how he had to get out; they both needed a breather and all of that. The fact that the hotel was just on the outskirts of Dublin and far from his mother's house made this line of reasoning very tricky. Backed into a corner, he eventually spilled everything but said it was the first time. That also turned out to be a lie by a long shot. It was really difficult telling the kids—they were teens and acting up anyway—but we sat them down and went through it. Funny thing was, after the initial shock, they started to take Nick's side, Sam particularly, and that was a bit of a double-whammy, but *what doesn't kill us makes us stronger*, so I doubled down on resilience and figured I just had to get through it and show my kids that there is always a way of burrowing through difficulty and seeing the light at the other side.

Looking over at Steve's house, I wondered what sort of reserves of resilience were going to be called on. So far, he just seemed like someone who was bringing something very different to the street. Maybe it was just something we would have to adapt to, and we'd reach some sort of détente. That was what I hoped, anyway, but when I returned from work that evening, that particular scenario looked a bit less likely.

Steve had added another car to the one he was fixing. This one was parked high up on the path directly outside his house. It was parked so high up that to walk past it, you would have to squeeze between it and his low-rider, which was on the street, or else squeeze between it and the wall at the front of Steve's house. Either way, it was a squeeze, and you would have to go out on the road entirely if you were pushing a buggy or in a wheelchair. This was clearly not acceptable. However, I didn't want to get straight into it, as I was tired after a day's work.

Cathy came down to hover in the kitchen as I was defrosting a chicken curry that I had thankfully thrown together and frozen the previous weekend.

'You want to do some rice and have a bit of curry with me?' I asked Cathy, and surprisingly, she went straight about the task of rinsing the basmati and putting it on. Cathy was prone to protesting in the form of prevarication and dawdling if she felt in any way put upon, and it was very easy to induce that state. Usually, just asking her to do something did the trick.

Fifteen minutes later, the two of us were sitting at the table, and the steaming, bready smell of basmati mixed with the spicy smell of the curry infused the room. I was beginning to unwind after the tension of a day's work.

'How'd you get on today?' I ventured.

'Good, yeah. Got a bit of work, which I badly need.'

'Oh yeah? Whereabouts?'

'That guy Steve has asked me to babysit his daughters tonight. He has custody of them a couple of nights a week, and he says it's the only time he can go to the gym.'

The smells in the room suddenly became less tantalizing. 'Oh? He just up and asked you, or how did that happen?'

'I was out looking for Tammy, and he just kind of saw me outside 'cos he was working on the cars, so he asked me.'

I wondered had she really been out looking for Tammy, our tabby cat, or was she out checking Steve out? After all, she had said he wasn't bad-looking. The babysitting offer put me in a bit of a conundrum. I had said to Cathy that a part-time job would be good for her, help with our stretched family finances, and it had been a bit of a bone of contention, but this was not what I had been thinking of. Steve definitely looked a bit rough around the edges.

'Well, I suppose you can try it and see how it goes.' I was buying time with that response, but I couldn't outright say no.

'Yeah, exactly, he seems pretty sound. I mean, I know he's a bit different to the people we usually have living here, but there's nothing wrong with that. We're all going to have to get used to living in mixed neighbourhoods. Lack of equality in society is what causes most of the problems. People want to live in their gilded ivory towers, and that's just not how life should be.'

I could feel a sociopolitical lecture coming on, so I left it at that. Hopefully, the kids would be a nightmare, and the dogs would scare her, and that would be that.

Fred called round later that evening. We both stood at the door and looked across at Steve's.

'He can't just breeze in and take over like that,' Fred said, pointing at the third car that was blocking the path.

'You're right, but maybe it's just for a short time. I suppose we have to give the guy a chance.'

As if on cue, Steve came marching out of his house, the two pit bulls straining at their chains, snarling at everything around them. He looked over at us and gave a wave. 'Just taking the mutts out for their walk. They have the garden torn up on me already.' He smiled ruefully at the two snarling brutes and continued up the road.

'It's a disgrace,' Fred said, shaking his head. 'A bloody disgrace.'

Just then, we saw my neighbour on the other side, Paul, emerge from his house to throw something in the bin. He looked over at us and hesitated before walking out his drive and up mine. He looked red-faced and was slightly out of breath. Paul had run a successful architecture firm, but rumour had it his appetite for drink had got the better of him, and the practice started a steady downward slide. I would have noticed myself even if he hadn't started coming home with bags of clinking bottles very early in the day. Now he worked mostly from home, doing design work on his PC and getting someone else to do all the client interaction.

'Been a few changes around.' Paul had developed a truncated style of communication to go with his increased tendency to slur words. Maybe he hoped people wouldn't notice if he kept the sentences short.

'Yes, there have, and they are certainly not changes for the better,' Fred said emphatically.

'We'll have to see how it goes,' I said in a more placatory tone. 'The letting agent told us to get in touch if we had any problems. He seems all right.'

'*If* we have any problems?' Fred intoned. 'Nothing but problems coming from that side anyway, I'd say. Those students in the other house don't seem too bad, but this guy, I can tell you he looks like trouble to me.'

We parted on that note, and an hour later, Cathy stuck her head in the living room's door. 'I'm off to do my babysitting gig. See you later.'

'All right, love. Look after yourself, and mind those dogs.'

'They're grand. He has them in a cage out the back most of the time.'

I watched her disappear out the door, and while I felt definite trepidation at seeing her work with someone like Steve, I also felt some admiration for the way she was willing to back up her own beliefs that we did need a more equal society, so she wasn't just going to treat people differently because they behaved differently.

Sam moseyed in a half hour later and peered into the fridge.

'There's some chicken curry that Cathy and I had left over. It's in a Tupperware.'

Sam didn't respond to that, but half the time, he had those ear pods in, and you couldn't see them because of his thick, curly hair, so I stood up to take a more direct approach.

'It's okay, Mam, I have it.' He withdrew the Tupperware, and I sat down again. I was vaguely watching news, bored by most of it but still hanging in there to see if anything of relevance came up. My work makes me interested in all things social and domestic. I keep a weather eye out for any moves or changes in policy, but also for incidents that may form the next case file that could land on my desk.

'Any news from the world of nineteen-year-olds?' I enquired.

Sam paused and stared down at his plate, as if the steaming mass of chicken curry had some secrets to divulge. 'Those guys are first years, engineers,' he said eventually, gesturing at the other house that had been rented to the students.

'Oh, funny time of year for them to be moving in. It's nearly end of term.'

'Think they got a good deal. That guy who was outside the other night is an uncle of one of them,' he said solemnly, lifting a forkful of curry. 'Philly. I walked back with him today.'

'Philly,' I repeated. 'I see. I hope he doesn't turn it into a party house.'

Sam didn't respond to that but lowered his head closer to the plate in an action I felt indicated he preferred to engage with his food over me.

Cathy arrived back at about one. I was already in bed but was listening out for her. A sense of relief flooded through me that she was back and obviously okay. I just hoped those babysitting gigs would be few and far between.

4

Things took a turn for the worse the next day. I arrived back from work in the evening to see Steve revving the car he was fixing in the drive. The other car was still blocking the path. I was tired after the day's work, so I hurried into the house and made myself a strong mug of coffee. I had just sat into an armchair in the living room when there was a knock on the door. I pulled it open to find Fred standing outside, his face reddening and what looked like a fleck of spittle at the side of his mouth.

Oh dear, I thought, *this doesn't look good.*

Steve definitely wasn't helping matters by revving the engine even louder. I looked over in his direction. He was standing outside the car, driver's door open, but his foot was inside and obviously pushing on the gas pedal. He had his head cocked to one side, presumably listening for something in the engine sound.

'It's a complete nuisance,' Fred said finally. 'This can't go on.'

Then, amazingly, Steve, who must have seen us standing at the door looking over at him, gave us a wave and a smile.

'That idiot. He has no idea how to behave. We have to get in contact with the agent.'

I walked Fred to the end of my driveway, hoping even that act would prove in some way calming. It didn't. He was shaking with anger. Paul came out and stood with us. Steve maintained his cheery demeanour, shrugging his shoulders towards us in a 'what you gonna do' kind of way and pointing at the car.

'Who does he think he is?' Paul asked no one in particular. 'He needs a good talking-to.'

I could see Paul had a couple of drinks on him and was afraid the situation might escalate.

'It's okay. I'll give that agent, McCann, a call. My ex has his number. I think it's best that we all go back to our houses for now, and I'll let you know how I get on.'

Both Fred and Paul hesitated, but they eventually went back to their respective houses. I got on the phone to Nick.

'Yeah?' He sounded surprised to hear from me.

'Do you have that guy McCann's number? The new neighbour with the cars is really getting people riled up here.'

'Oh.' Nick sounded noncommittal. 'Are you sure it's that bad that you need to call him? Can you not have a word yourselves?'

'That's exactly what I'm trying to avoid. Fred and Paul are both pretty worked up. That guy Steve seems pretty tough. It's better to go through official channels.'

'But I'm supposed to start working for McCann, like, next week, and money is kind of tight.'

'That's got nothing to do with it. We live here. You don't.'

A short silence from the other end was followed by a sigh. 'Okay, then.' He called the number out reluctantly.

I dialled as soon as we hung up. The phone rang for a few long seconds; then I heard a tentative, 'Hello, Jim McCann.'

'Hi, Jim, sorry to call you in the evening. It's June Sweeney here. I was talking to you the other day. It's about our new neighbour, Steve Murray. He's making a nuisance of himself with those cars, blocking footpaths and revving engines at all times of the day.'

'Oh, I'm sorry about that. I had a word with him before he moved in that he'd have to respect the area. I'll give him a call and get back to you.'

I had my doubts that he'd call back, but ten minutes later, my phone rang.

'June, I've had a word with him, and he's promised to tone it down. He says he's waiting for proper premises and should have the whole thing sorted soon.'

I stood by my window and looked across at Steve's house. He had indeed stopped working on the car. All was quiet over at his place.

'Okay, he seems to have stopped, but my elderly neighbour, Fred, is getting very worked up, and I'm just worried that he might take matters into his own hands.'

'That's exactly what we want to avoid, isn't it? You did the right thing by calling me. I'll keep a close eye on the situation.'

I had a peaceful evening after that. Sam was out, and Cathy was staying over at a friend's, so it was just me and Tammy, our cat, hanging out. I poured myself a glass of wine and stuck a Spotify playlist on. I had an eclectic mix of oldies, country and western, and electronic music that I'd picked up along the way, all chosen for soft melodies, music that you can really sink into. Tammy sat beside me, purring gently like an engine that is slowly switching off. The spring evening was starting to close in with that thickening light that gives the shapes around you a bulkier appearance.

I must have fallen asleep because I woke to the sound of a key scratching in the door. This was followed by the light suddenly springing on and startling me. I must have looked shocked or something because Sam, who had just opened the door, stood there for a few seconds looking at me.

'What are you doing?' he said eventually.

'I must have fallen asleep. Where were you?'

'Just across the road in that new guy, Philly's, house.' He started making his way to the kitchen, where I saw him stick a full pizza into the oven.

'Hungry?'

'Yeah, starving.'

His voice was slower than usual, and when he turned towards me, his eyes were red at the sides. He wasn't slurring at all, though, so I reckoned he hadn't really been drinking, which made me think he might have been smoking weed. I knew kids that age got up to whatever they got up to, and I didn't rule with an iron fist as long as it didn't interfere with the other, more important aspects of their lives. In Sam's case, that was college and the sports scholarship. It had proven a financial boon to us, as they'd paid his fees and thrown a bit of spending money on top because he was a super footballer.

'Okay, love, I'm off to bed. Do you want me to call you in the morning?'

'No, Mam, I'll get myself up,' he said with a tinge of teenage irritation.

'Okay, okay, just asking. Night.'

Unfortunately, that turned out not to be the case, as he was still fast asleep by the time I'd had breakfast and was ready to go out the door, so I had no option but to give a couple of raps on the door and wait until I heard him shuffling around inside.

Next evening, I was filled with a sense of dread as I pulled into my estate, but to my absolute joy, one of the cars that Steve had been working on had gone, and the one that was blocking the path was now in his driveway. That felt like a little victory. Maybe Jim McCann's talking to him had done the trick.

I rustled up a vegetarian curry from the extra veg that seemed to be accumulating in the veg basket. I see it as a handy way of tidying up, just throw all the veg in with a bit of curry powder and some coconut milk, and hey, presto! Cathy must have caught the smells because she emerged from her bedroom and got some plates and cutlery out.

'I'm babysitting again for Steve,' she announced. 'I saw him on the road today, and he asked me.'

'Oh, that's nice,' I said with as much conviction as I could muster. I was hoping the babysitting thing would be something very occasional. Maybe it was just a busy week for Steve.

'Yeah, I could do with the money. The girls are talking about getting an Airbnb in Lisbon for a couple of weeks this summer. They all have part-time jobs, so they have a bit saved.'

'Well, I did encourage you to get a job before they were all swallowed up by other students last September.'

'Yes, I know, Mam. No need to go over that for, like, the millionth time. I did go around, just I have no experience, so they wouldn't take me.'

Cathy had made a token effort of going around to a few cafés and shops, but I suspected at the time it wasn't just the lack of experience that made them hesitate. Cathy is a strong, opinionated young woman, and maybe they'd thought she could be a bit lippy with customers.

Sam bustled in the door then, threw his sports bag in the hall, and joined us at the table. I was glad to see he'd made it to class and just hoped he didn't get in the habit of going over to Philly's to smoke; otherwise I would have to have a talk with him.

I did a little gardening later, snipped at some roses that

had grown with remarkable speed over the last couple of weeks. They were starting to throw their weight around, threatening to overshadow some of the smaller plants. I love roses when they flower, but you can't forget that they have these long stems with very sharp thorns on them. I tried to remember which fairy tale, or were there multiple fairy tales, where someone goes to pick a rose and gets pricked by a thorn for their trouble? *Ah, well, doesn't matter now; it won't be happening to me*, I thought as I used my pruning snips to cut off a couple of meaty-looking stems. I paused then to enjoy looking up the estate in the fading light of a calm spring evening. A blackbird was standing on a chimney nearby, proclaiming with its melodic trilling that this was its territory. *Looking for a mate, too*, I supposed, it being springtime. We had quite a few privet hedges that served as borders between houses, and I would frequently see blackbirds flitting in and out of these. I would also see the occasional fox stroll boldly up the road, a reminder that not so many years ago this area was mostly green fields and woodland. It was an estate I had come to love over the years I had lived there—peaceful and natural. I sincerely hoped it would stay that way.

Sam stayed in because he had an assignment due the next day, so I furnished him with some tea and a toasted cheese sandwich around ten and started getting ready for bed. I read the paper in bed, some article about a celebrity couple who were going through a very public separation, and it led me to think of my own situation. I didn't dwell on it much, but sometimes the big double bed seemed awfully big. I hadn't gone back on any dating scene since separating from Nick and had studiously avoided the dating apps, but I sometimes felt like putting a toe in the water. I thought of McCann and his broad, handsome face and his warm, dry hands and wondered if he was married. With those thoughts, I drifted into sleep, the bedside light still on beside me. I woke a couple of hours later and checked my watch. Two a.m. I decided to go for a pee before going back to sleep, so I went quietly to the toilet, not wanting to wake Sam if he'd been up late working on the assignment. However, when I hit the landing, I noticed that Cathy's door was still open. If she was home, her door was always firmly closed to block out all the irritations of the domestic world around her.

That's funny, I thought, *she's very late. Where the hell could Steve be till this hour, and is Cathy going to be able to get up for college in the morning?*

I took a peek out the window in Cathy's room, which has a view directly across to Steve's. I could see the low-rider car he had arrived in the first day and the other car he was working on, so it looked like he was home.

I went back to bed, feeling very uncomfortable about the whole thing, but maybe he hadn't taken his car out, and maybe I was getting unnecessarily worked up about it, but I just didn't like the idea of Cathy getting embroiled with someone like Steve. I decided we'd have to chat about it the next day.

5

As it happened, I noticed that Steve had reinstated another car in his drive, so he was back to having three outside his house by the time I returned from work the next day. He was in overalls and working chirpily on one of them. The car door was open, as it was last time, but this time he had added blaring music from the car stereo to the other inconveniences. He gave me a wave as I pulled in and made some sort of show of turning the music down, but in truth, it went just from mega-decibels to nearly mega-decibels. Again, I just wanted to get indoors and get a bit of food inside me, so I trudged on in and stuck a couple of packets of tortellini in boiling water. I heated up a bit of tomato and basil sauce and within ten minutes had a presentable dinner on the table. I shouted upstairs, and both children trooped down to join me.

Sam looked across in the direction of Steve's house as soon as he sat.

'It's kind of hard getting stuff done with that racket going on out there.'

'I can imagine it is, dear. I called the agent, Jim McCann,

the other night about all the cars, but it hasn't made much impact.'

'It's how he makes his living,' Cathy said truculently.

'I know it is, love, but he has to respect other people's privacy and their right to have a bit of peace and quiet.'

'It's just because everyone is so old and judgemental on this street.'

'Sam's not old.'

'Well, he's being a bit judgemental. I mean, the guy has a right to play a bit of music while he works. Better than being some layabout who's scrounging off the state.'

'I am not being judgemental. You were giving out about someone drilling up the road a couple of weeks ago.'

'That was when I had, like, four hours to finish an assignment.'

'You're not the only one with assignments to finish.'

There was a pause as they gave their tortellini renewed attention.

'Was Steve back late last night?'

'Oh, is it going to be the Steve inquisition tonight, or can we actually sit down and have a bit of food without all this fuss?'

'I was just asking because you were late back, and you had school this morning.'

'I made it to college this morning, in case you didn't notice.'

I hadn't noticed because I was gone to work, but I wasn't about to say that. 'That's good you made it, just you don't want it being a regular thing, out late during the week.'

'Mam, I'm twenty. I can look after myself.'

I think Cathy had first said that to me when she was eighteen, and although an independent person, she did need strong nudges in the right direction. In terms of the babysitting, I felt she was being defensive, but if I'd learned anything over the years, it was not to be confrontational because the kids just clam up, and you get absolutely nothing out of them then. It was something I hoped would just run out of steam of its own accord.

The music was still going strong at eight o'clock. There was a knock on my door. Fred was there in a renewed state of agitation.

'It's just not on. We have to do something.'

'I called the agent two days ago, and I think that's why we got that brief lull.'

'We're going to have to have a strong word with him ourselves.'

Paul emerged from his house, perhaps having seen the two of us standing in the drive. He was red-faced again and looked to be unsteady on his feet.

'Bloody disgrace,' he said when he reached us. 'Bloody disgrace. Who does he think he is?'

'I was saying we need to sort this out ourselves,' Fred said, his head shaking with anger.

'I'm not so sure it's a good idea for the three of us to march over there. That might just provoke him,' I ventured. 'Maybe just one of us should go over.'

'I'll go,' Paul said. 'I've had enough.'

'No, I don't think that's a good idea,' I said quickly, but Paul was already marching unsteadily over.

The scene that unfolded happened in slow motion. From the moment Paul left us, I had a chill feeling of dread in the pit of my stomach. He was all tensed up with rage, but at the same time, he lurched from side to side as he made his way across.

Steve seemed initially oblivious. He was polishing a chrome fitting that he had detached and was nodding his head to the music. He lifted his head and smiled as he saw

Paul start up his short driveway. He kept on polishing the fitting.

I went after Paul, fearing what might happen next. My main concern was to get him out of there. We could decide what to do about Steve another time. Unfortunately, I was too late.

Paul had marched right up to Steve, so he was standing just inches away from him. Steve put the fitting down on the bonnet of the car. He was still smiling, though, and I saw him back away a little and flick at his overalls like something had landed there. I figured Paul had probably let a bit of spittle fly in his rage.

I had reached the end of Steve's drive when I saw Paul start to poke him in the chest. He was shouting as well, but it was hard to hear what he was saying with the loud music and Paul's slurring speech. Steve backed away again, but the smile had vanished. I could see his shoulders tensing up. Paul came at him again, and this time, Steve gave him a shove that knocked him back a few feet. I went further up the drive to try to grab Paul, shouting his name as I went, but he didn't turn around. Instead, he lunged at Steve, and I could see an unsteady fist sailing through the air towards Steve's face. Steve stepped back another step and easily blocked the punch with his right arm, but at the same time, he drew his left back and flashed a lightning-quick jab straight into Paul's face.

Paul staggered back, holding his nose, which had an immediate stream of blood pumping from it. He stopped, and I thought he was going to go back again and swing for Steve, so I grabbed his jacket and pulled him down the drive.

'C'mon, Paul, it's over. Let's get out of here,' I said as I pulled him. He was still doubled over, and I could hear him groaning with pain. Steve stood where he was and watched us. The expression on his face was cold and hard, but he made no move to follow Paul.

'You need to turn that music down,' I shouted at him as we left. I could feel my own blood boiling. He stayed where he was for a few seconds, then leaned into the car and turned the music down a few notches.

'All you had to do was ask,' he said, the smile creeping back onto his face.

I helped Paul back to my house and laid him out on the couch. Fred had come in too and was dancing nervously around him.

'Oh, God, what did he do to you? I can tell you he hasn't heard the last of this.'

I got a bag of ice from the freezer and pressed it against the injury. His nose was swollen where he'd been hit, but it didn't look like it was broken.

'I'll get onto Jim McCann,' I said. 'He needs to sort this out.'

'We need to get onto the police,' Fred said. 'That was an assault just there.'

I shook my head. I'd been long enough around families in crisis and situations that had spiralled out of control. 'The police won't have anything to do with this. Paul went onto his property and threw the first punch. Unfortunately, that's the way the law is going to see it.'

'But we just can't go on like this. He's ruining our street.'

Paul was happy to hobble back to his house after the blood had stopped pouring and the swelling had gone down. He wasn't as animated as Fred, and I guessed it was probably because he knew he was in the wrong. He shouldn't have gone in and started getting physical with Steve.

I gave Jim McCann a call once they had both gone. Fred had pretty much laid it down as a condition for leaving. He wanted action, but I wasn't convinced he was going to get it.

McCann was polite, but he got me to describe the order of events, and as I did, I could hear a tone of ambivalence creeping in.

He concluded on a conciliatory but not very satisfactory note.

'Thanks again for calling me, June. It really helps to know what's going on with the tenants, and I will speak to Mr Murray again, but by the sounds of it, there was some provocation involved. If we're going to resolve this, we have to be really careful. You know the way people are so up to speed on their rights these days. As the letting agent, I don't want to end up in court, nor do any of your neighbours. But, and I mean this, we will do our best to sort this out.'

I wasn't exactly satisfied with the outcome when I hung up. McCann was making himself out to have limited powers in what he could do about Steve, who didn't seem like someone who was going to roll over easily. It looked like we were being left to ourselves, to a certain extent, and that wasn't good news. Both Fred and Paul were vulnerable in their own ways, and I was a woman, on my own, trying to complete the job of raising two kids. I just wanted to get back to the peace and calm we had enjoyed before.

6

I spent the day in work trying to sort out the case of a girl who had been brought into the country apparently as a marriage arrangement. Problem was she was only fifteen, so too young to marry in our jurisdiction, not helped by the fact that she could speak very little English and contact with her family, who lived abroad, was very difficult. We had to get a translator in, and that was going to take a few hours before we got the right one, so meanwhile, I was just left waiting while the girl was kept in a secure environment. I decided to use the time to see if I could find anything out about Steve. He'd mentioned that there was a custody battle going on with his ex, so that meant there would be a file. It took a bit of time, but I eventually found it. The case was pending in the courts. A date had been set for a few weeks' time, but reading through the reason for the separation and the ex's objection to his having custody, I came across a string of convictions and some jail time that Steve had previously served for a number of different offences. He'd been done for assault, possession with intent to supply, aggravated assault, obstruction of justice and so on, all of which painted a

picture of a volatile and out-of-control man. I wondered if Jim
McCann had been aware of all these charges when he let the
house to Steve. Maybe he found out too late and had no
appetite for confronting someone as dangerous as Steve. That
was certainly the way I felt when I read through the charge
sheets. We were going to have to be very careful with him, but
at the same time, we couldn't back down.

Nick's pickup was outside my house when I got back, and
I have to say that didn't help my mood. In work I had
managed to sort the girl through some arduous translation,
and she was being kept in secure accommodation until we
managed to get her safely back to her country of origin. It was
a case that would probably play out for weeks as we liaised
with embassy and immigration people. I felt tired after the
day of wrangling.

'Had a hard day? Me too.' Nick was sitting at the wooden
dining table with a steaming mug of coffee in front of him. He
was looking out towards the estate in a proprietorial manner.
'Did a fair bit of work on the two rented houses there. That
one with the students needed serious work in the back.' He
checked his hands like they might have suffered some
damage from the hard labour he had put them through.

I poured the remains of the coffee jug into a mug and
stuck it in the microwave. It was only after taking a few sips of
coffee that I felt ready for Nick.

'That's good that you got going, anyway.' That was about
as much enthusiasm as I could muster.

'Yeah, McCann says the landlord is actively looking for
property in the area, so there's a promise of plenty more work
to come, but even between those two houses, I'll be kept
going for a while.'

The prospect of Nick hovering in the vicinity for any
protracted period of time didn't exactly fill me with joy.

'That's great.'

Nick gave me a slightly hurt look. 'You don't sound too enthusiastic.'

'I'm tired after a long day at work. It takes time to wind down, as I'm sure you know.'

'Yeah, well, it doesn't hurt to show a bit of interest. The money earned is for all of us.'

'The money I earn is for all of us as well, but I'm not going on about it. By the way, how did you get in?'

'Oh, so I have to explain myself, do I?'

'Well, when we split, that was the agreement, separate living places unless by prior arrangement.'

'Sam, my son, let me in.'

He almost spat the words 'my son'. 'Right, just asking so we can be clear about things. You can let yourself out, then, when you're done.' I had had enough, so I took my coffee up to my room, where I could at least shut the door and start to unwind properly.

I sat and stared out my bedroom window. It looked across some unused grassland that backed on to the college campus behind. This was the area that planning permission requests for the big block of student accommodation had been put in. If they had got their way, I would currently be looking right at a newly constructed, four-storey student hall. This was what Fred and I had resisted so strongly, as it is our houses that back right onto that land. I was so glad we had won and could at least savour the view out into the open space. I heard the door close downstairs and expected to hear Nick's pickup start up, but I didn't. Instead, I heard the sound of voices chatting. I sneaked over to Cathy's room, which had a view out onto the estate. The door was open, so I knew she wasn't in. Looking out her window, I saw Nick standing at the end of Steve's driveway, and the two of them were holding a loud conversation as Steve worked away at one of the cars.

Oh, God, I thought, *don't tell me the two of them are getting friendly.*

I heard Nick's pickup taking off a few minutes later and ventured to the window to see Steve working on his cars, but without the music this time. The second car was still blocking half the path, but I was grateful that at least the noise part had died down. Neither Fred nor Paul came out for the next couple of days, so I took it they were happy that at least the noise had gone too.

Cathy did another babysitting gig and came home well after Steve's car came back. I was in bed but couldn't sleep, but I decided to say nothing this time after the last confrontation. It could be something completely harmless, I tried to convince myself.

A strange thing happened then on the Saturday afternoon of that week. I was in and out of the house doing the garden, messing on my phone, just whiling away the time and trying to forget about the week gone by. Nick wasn't around, which was a relief because he'd been in and out of the estate quite a bit. Steve had been a presence in his driveway but kept to himself and kept the music down. I did see him at one point dragging his vicious dogs up the road. They looked exactly like the caged animals they were, straining at their metal chains with the first hint of freedom.

I think I was scrolling mindlessly through Facebook when there was a knock on my front door. When I opened it, a respectable-looking couple in their late thirties were standing there smiling. I was pretty sure I'd never seen them before, but their smiles threw me and made me scratch the inner recesses of memory, but I couldn't come up with anything.

He was dressed in a Polo shirt and jeans while she was in a blouse and a dark-coloured skirt. They looked as normal and as pedestrian as any couple could look, yet something about them was off. Maybe it was the holes from piercings I could see in his earlobes. They looked fresh, like the earrings had been recently taken out, or maybe it was the lines at the side of her eyes that gave them a lived-in look, but immediately, my antennae were up. Something about the way they were dressed and the way they actually looked as people didn't compute. My years as a social worker had equipped me with probably more street smarts than I would actually want to have, but I had developed that sixth sense with people over the years.

'How are you?' she gushed as I looked at them. '*So* sorry for interrupting your Saturday afternoon, but myself and Eamon were down to look at a house around the corner, and we just strolled into your estate, and you really have a nice set-up here. Stephanie, by the way.' She reached out for a handshake, which I gave in as brisk a manner as possible.

'We're really interested in this area,' Eamon concurred, 'so we just had to take a look around here.'

I wasn't sure where this was all going, so I just nodded in agreement.

'The thing is,' Stephanie said, looking all coquettish all of a sudden, 'we know it's cheeky, but we were wondering if you know if anyone's thinking of selling up. We wanted to get in before the estate agents get their claws in and start driving prices up.'

'Not that I know of,' I replied quickly.

'Oh, and you're not thinking of selling yourself?' Eamon asked.

'No, not at all.'

'Oh, right, because we're cash customers, and we'd give a good price,' she said, moving from coquettish to businesslike in the blink of an eye.

'No, sorry to disappoint.' With that, I started closing the door.

'Okay, but if you change your mind, here's my number.'

Stephanie handed me a slip of paper with a mobile number on it and her name, which was written just as *Stephanie* with no surname.

My God, that was weird, I thought when I had closed the door on them, the whole thing about their being so gracious yet pushy at the same time and how their appearance had been slightly off. I made myself a strong cup of tea and kept checking up the road to make sure they weren't coming back.

I dropped into Fred later on that evening to tell him they had been around. He wasn't surprised. They had called in to him too.

'They seemed like a nice couple,' he had said, 'but I have no intention of moving. I've lived here all my life. Margaret and I had many happy memories here before she passed away. A house is much more than a place you just live in. It becomes a part of you. That's how I feel about it, anyway.'

Fred was usually quite a reserved person, someone who had been a great neighbour but at the same time kept to himself, so I was a bit surprised when he came out with that. As I walked home, I thought that all the changes on the road must be really getting to him. He sounded like he was really digging the heels in, almost like he was getting ready for a fight.

7

S am, Cathy and I were settling in for dinner the next evening when I spotted Nick and Jim McCann walking slowly towards the house. They seemed to be deep in conversation, chatting about work, I presumed. To my surprise, both of them came in my short driveway, and next thing, Nick was ringing the bell.

When I answered, Nick stepped inside the hallway. McCann stayed outside.

'I hope things have improved with Mr Murray,' he said, looking across the way to where Steve just had one car in the drive and one on the road. He wasn't out working on either, and I couldn't hear either loud music or the dogs.

'I guess things have quietened down a bit, but that was a very unpleasant altercation the other evening. I know he didn't throw the first punch, but still, we've never had anything like that happen on our road.'

'And never will again, I hope,' McCann said quickly. He was smiling at me, and he had a warmth in his eyes that made you want to believe whatever he was saying. 'Nick and I were just finalizing the work that needs to be done for the week. Quite a bit, in fact. This ex of yours is a good worker.'

Nick looked almost bashful when McCann said that. 'It's nice to get stuck into something,' he said.

McCann turned around and started to leave but flashed a warm smile in my direction as he did. 'If there's anything I can do for you, be sure to let me know.'

Nick continued into the hall after McCann left, and I thought to myself, *I don't remember inviting him in*, but he had already gone in to say hello to the kids, putting the kettle on at the same time. He got himself a mug of tea and sat down.

'Here, Dad, there's some leftovers.' Cathy got up and got a little lamb stew and potatoes, heated it in the microwave, and slid it in front of Nick.

'Dinner and everything. I really wasn't expecting that, but I guess it's been a long day, so the bit of grub is very welcome.'

'You and McCann seem quite friendly now,' I said.

'Yeah, he's a good guy, just trying to make a few bucks like the rest of us. I know the other guy, Steve, seems a bit off for this neighbourhood, but I'm sure he'll settle in. I hear he's looking for a premises, so that'll sort the car thing if he gets one.'

'So I've heard, but I haven't seen any movement yet.'

'Mom isn't a big fan of Steve's, as you may have noticed,' Cathy said with a wry smile.

'He did smack poor Paul on the nose. I'm all for people doing their own thing, but not when it's a provocation.'

'He's just fixing cars. How is that a provocation?'

'Loud music, working at all times of day and night.'

'Give the guy a chance,' Nick said. 'I'm sure he'll be okay in the end.'

'Yeah, Mam,' Sam chimed in. 'You need to give people a chance.'

That kind of stung, but I bit my tongue and said nothing.

Sam probably felt he had to say something, and I wondered if he was talking about my split with Nick. Did he feel that I hadn't given Nick a 'chance'? Because nothing could be further from the truth. Nick had always been quite self-centred, but I had learned to live with it for the sake of family harmony and so our kids could have a pleasant living environment.

'Anyway, here's to better times. I'll be around a good bit more, I guess. Might need somewhere to leave the tools. Don't want to be dragging them around with me all the time.'

I chose to ignore that comment. I wasn't sure if Nick was looking for the keys to the house or what, but I had no intention of finding out.

Sam went over to Philly's house after dinner, and Cathy went out with some friends, so I was left alone once Nick disappeared.

There was a knock on the door about nine o'clock. I was surprised to see Steve standing there. He had his overalls on and had something of a cheeky grin on his face when I answered.

'Listen, hope everything is okay after the other night. That wasn't meant to happen, but the guy just started swinging at me, and the old instincts kicked in.'

'Yeah, he was pretty shook up after it. I haven't really seen him out since.' I wasn't going to play the incident down.

'These things happen, but we should all be able to get along. You gave McCann a call about it.'

He posed that more as a statement than a question.

'Of course I did. And I called him about the mess that the cars are making outside. It's actually a bit of a hazard the way you sometimes park them half up on the footpath. What about wheelchair users or elderly people?'

Steve's cheeky grin had completely disappeared, and that hard look I had seen just after he punched Paul had taken its place. I was nervous, but I was determined to stand my ground.

'Give a guy a break. I'm looking for premises. These things take time. I'm not a magician. I have to put bread on the table in the meantime. Hungry mouths to feed. You know the score.'

'I do. I've been doing it for years.'

'Well, there you go. Besides, it looks like I have a couple of aces up the sleeves now.'

'Meaning?'

He grinned, but this time there was a sinister edge to it. His mouth moved, but his eyes stayed cold. 'Meaning your family members think more highly of me than you do. In fact, one of them thinks very highly of me indeed.'

'What exactly do you mean by that? I sincerely hope you are not playing games with members of my family.'

'Not games as such. Nothing she isn't willing to partici- pate in herself. She's a grown woman, in case you hadn't noticed.'

I tried to hide the shock I was feeling at what he was saying, but I must have gone pale. I could feel waves of anxiety rushing through my stomach. The only thing I wanted to do was close that door and be rid of his grinning face, but I didn't want to give him that satisfaction.

'You need to watch your step here. You have your rights as a tenant, but we have our rights too, and believe me, we will use them.'

'We? I wonder who that is. Looks to me like you're on your own now, unless you count the old fella and the alco. I wouldn't fancy them as much of a team.'

Steve turned and strolled slowly down my drive. I closed the door heavily after him. I was shaking after the encounter, part anger and part fear. What the hell was he trying to do to me, and why?

I waited for Cathy to come home. She was late. Sam came back before her, and he had a big grin plastered all over his face. I saw him reach into the fridge and grab two chocolate yoghurts, which he brought up to his room. I wasn't in the humour to pull him up or ask what he had been up to. I needed to steel myself for the encounter with Cathy.

She spilled in the door about one in the morning with her bag and jacket hanging off her. She looked like someone who'd been out on the town, but she was humming to herself, as she still had her ear pods in. She made a beeline for the fridge and a glass of orange juice, and it was only then she noticed me sitting in the corner and gave me a wave before taking her ear pods out.

'You're up late for a working day.'

I usually tried to turn in around eleven, read a bit and fall into a gentle sleep so I'd be in form for what the day would throw at me.

'Yeah, I wanted to talk to you about something, but have your juice and hang your jacket up or whatever you need to do.'

'Sounds serious.' Cathy ignored my previous suggestion and plonked herself in an armchair opposite me.

'I'm not sure how serious it is, but it's something I'd like to nip in the bud before it does get serious, if you get me.'

'Maybe. I'm not sure what it's all about, am I?'

A hint of defiance was already creeping into her tone.

'It's about Steve and the babysitting and maybe for you to tell me if there's anything more to it.'

Cathy sat straight up, looking very together and sober all of a sudden. 'How do you mean "anything more"?'

'I mean exactly that. You've arrived home late a couple of times, well after his car has reappeared, and I was wondering what the delays were about.'

'Delays,' Cathy spat the word.

'Well, call them what you will. To cut to the chase, what I
want to know is if there's any involvement between the two of
you that goes beyond the babysitting?'

Cathy looked down at the bag that was in her lap before
looking up at me again. 'We get on, if that's what you mean,
and he is a good-looking guy. He's different from the college
guys, speaks his mind, and well, he's less of a pushover.'

'So there is something between you?' I could feel my
heart racing, but I held the arm of the chair to steady myself.

'I don't know if you would call it "something", but we get
along. I think he finds me attractive, and the feeling is
mutual.'

'But Cathy, you know he has been making quite a
nuisance of himself since he arrived with his cars and his
music and his dogs. The other night, he hit Paul when he
challenged him.'

'He said that Paul went for him. It was self-defence.'

'Oh, so he talked to you about it?'

Cathy shook her head, and I could hear whatever beads
she had around her neck rattle with the movement.

'Mom, it's not that big a deal. It's just because we live in
this cossetted, bourgeois kind of fantasy world where
everyone has to be nice and polite to each other. That's not
the way the world works. He reacted to something someone
did to him, and maybe his reactions are stronger than what
we're used to around here, but it's over now.'

'Cathy, this is a world that you have grown up securely in
and has allowed you to develop securely and become the
person that you are. It's not cossetted, it's a world that we have
deliberately chosen, and I for one don't want it to change.'

Cathy said nothing. She started playing with the bag on
her lap.

'Cathy, I looked into his background after that incident

with Paul, and he has a criminal past. He has served time in jail.'

'Oh, so you're snooping now. That's great, Mom. Nosy neighbour. Great. That stuff was in the past, and he wants to move on. He's been judged by society once. He doesn't need to be judged again.'

'I'm not judging him, but I am concerned for your well-being. You are my daughter, and although you're an adult, he is much older, and I would not be happy with him as an influence in your life.'

Cathy shook her head again. 'I appreciate your concern, Mam, but as you say, I am an adult and can make my own decisions. To me, he's someone who deserves a second chance, whatever that involves. Good night, Mam.'

Cathy gathered herself and made her way upstairs. I felt suddenly breathless and deflated. She had her side of the argument, and I could see it was going to be very hard to shift her. Cathy was incredibly stubborn at the best of times, and to me, this was certainly not the best of times.

8

There was no babysitting at Steve's for the next couple of days, which meant Cathy and I could have a détente of sorts. Steve, however, was not for having any détente. He had the cars out and the music on quite loud, not quite blaring the way he had it before, but loud enough so it was a nuisance.

Nick was around quite a lot and dropping in for the odd cup of tea when I wasn't there. Both Sam and Cathy had alluded to it. I didn't pass comment, although I would have preferred if he wasn't. Presumably, this gardening gig would last for an intense flurry and then die down.

However, one evening when he was knocking around and actually asked himself in for a cup of tea before going home, I decided to broach the subject of Steve and Cathy.

'You seem quite chatty with Steve across the way.'

Nick looked at me like I had accused him of something, but I kept my expression as neutral, curious and open as I could.

'Yeah, he's not a bad guy. Been through some tough times, but I think he's trying to turn a corner.'

'That's kind of what Cathy was saying about him.'

'Cathy?'

'Yes, she's been babysitting and, I suspect, getting in some way involved with him.'

I could see Nick stiffen. He took a tentative sip from the fresh mug of tea and reached for a plain biscuit from a packet that he must have brought in earlier. He dunked the biscuit in the tea and waited till it reached the right level of saturation before rushing it into his mouth. I watched this little display and wondered if he was trying to buy time and consider how to react.

Nick had perfected the art of fence-sitting in our later years together. He would do almost nothing or make almost no decision that might antagonize either Cathy or Sam. This, I figured in hindsight, was because he knew the affair would probably be discovered at some stage and that I would blow him out, so he wanted to keep the other two family members on board.

'I suppose she is an adult now, although he is a good deal older.' He did his best to look concerned as he imparted this.

'Did you know he has a fairly extensive criminal record and has done time?'

'Well, he alluded to a dodgy past, but I didn't get into the specifics.'

'The specifics are that he did time for a variety of criminal offences from drugs to assault, so he seems like a lower-rung criminal who can turn his hand to whatever comes up. Does that colour your perception of his suitability at all?'

Nick reached for another biscuit, dunked it, and lifted it to his mouth, but part of it fell back into is tea, so he started fishing for it with a teaspoon. I was beginning to get impatient with what I saw as foot-dragging.

'I know it's not ideal,' he said once he had fished the piece of biscuit out, 'but as I said, she is an adult, so what can we actually do about it? Besides, maybe it's just a friendship. It might be good for Cathy to branch out, away from the student bubble.'

'Well, I think we need to monitor the situation closely. I have already spoken to her and didn't get a very good reception.'

Nick shook his head and smiled. 'She is very pig-headed when she gets going, but that's an attribute that will serve her well in later life, you know, determination.'

'Not if it means getting caught up with a career criminal. We are her parents. She still needs guidance. I think you should talk to her. She thinks I'm just on her case, being the bossy mum. She isn't used to you being on her case about anything, so she might listen to you.'

Just then, the front door opened, and Sam came in. He poured a glass of milk, took a couple of Nick's biscuits, and sat at the table.

'What's going on in the world of the young?' Nick asked.

Sam shrugged. 'Same old, same old.'

'I love the way you guys have all these expressions that don't actually mean anything but serve as kind of conversational fillers, like "whatever" or "literally" or whatever the word of the day is.'

Sam shrugged again and took another biscuit.

'Or I suppose the nonverbals will do,' Nick said with a laugh.

'You were working at Philly's today?' Sam asked.

'Yeah, doing quite a lot around here now. Which brings me a to a bit of a sticky point. I could seriously do with somewhere to store tools and equipment to save me dragging them all around in the truck. It'd be nice to be able to pop in for tea or coffee or whatever on breaks too, so I was wondering if I could get spare keys to the house just for a little while. Jim McCann had suggested it, actually.'

It took me a few seconds to realise that this request was being directed at me because Nick was looking into a space somewhere between Sam and me.

'Keys?'

'Yeah, just for a bit. It'd be really handy.'

'There's usually someone here at different stages of the day, so you could just time it around that.'

'Well, it'd be handier if I had keys; then I wouldn't be bothering anyone or holding them to times or whatever.'

'I'll have a think about it.'

I didn't want to give Nick an answer in front of Sam, as I was pretty sure he had timed the question so either Sam or Cathy would be there and it'd be harder for me to say no. Also, I was dubious that Jim McCann would come out with something like that. Maybe he had said something about storing tools, but why would he go and pick my house specifically?

'Why not, Mam? If it's only for a while,' Sam said. I could see Nick nodding in agreement.

'I said I'd think about it.' I could hear a tone of irritation in my voice. This looked very like an ambush to me. Nick was a master at manipulating situations to his own advantage.

'But it's Dad. Why wouldn't you give him keys?'

That was a question I didn't want to have to answer because it dragged me into places I would very much like to forget about. I could have said, *well, it might be something to do with the fact that he deceived all of us for a number of years with someone who was a very good friend of mine and whom he is now shacked up with*, but I didn't. At the time of the split, it had been so difficult to explain to Sam and Cathy, who were bang in the middle of their teens. I did my utmost to paint it in the light of one of those life things that 'happen' because I genuinely didn't want them to think their dad was a bad person. My priority was to preserve their sense that they belonged to a loving family that was going through a difficulty that would eventually find a harmonious resolution. Looking across at Nick, I was reminded what a difficult and ongoing task that was.

'Okay, you can have a spare set, but just for a while.'

Nick smiled and nodded, obviously glad the outcome had been positive for him. When I looked at his thinning, dark hair and still boyish frame, I could reconstruct the person I had fallen for many years before, just with thicker, darker hair and more of the devil-may-care attitude he had sported so openly back then. Little did I know how truly devil-may-care he was to become. Now, I saw in him someone who was used to charming his way into getting what he wanted, but I saw nothing appealing in the charm, just a played-out self-interest that had very little that was attractive about it.

'Grand. I'd better get going, then.' Nick lifted the remains of the biscuit packet and stuck it in his jacket pocket; then he paused and fished them back out again. 'I suppose I'll be in and out tomorrow again.' He put the half-packet back on the table and left.

Sam and I were left at the table together in silence. I was about to get up and go watch TV when Sam turned to me.

'You always give Dad a hard time. He's just doing his best. Why would you make such a big deal out of a spare key? He did live here once, you know.'

That kind of took me by surprise. Sam was the type who kept things to himself, and although I had noticed an uptick in the brooding, I didn't expect that level of reaction to Nick's request.

'I try my very best not to give Nick a hard time precisely because he is your father, and I want you to have the respect for him as a dad that he deserves.'

'You've got a funny way of showing it.'

Again, that rattled me. Was he talking just about the key,

or was there a whole slew of incidents that were on his mind? I struggled to think of anything else in recent history.

'I do it the best that I can. As you know, we had our difficulties. I wanted you guys to have as normal a life as possible, so I tried to just get on with things. Maybe I didn't always manage that perfectly, but I tried.'

Sam rubbed his forehead. His curly locks dropped over his face. He wasn't making eye contact with me. I could sense a real restlessness coming off him, like there was something bigger going on in his mind.

'Dad's a good guy,' he said eventually. 'People make mistakes.'

'I know that. I make mistakes. We all do, but what happened had to happen because your dad and I couldn't keep living under the same roof. What led to that wasn't my choice.'

'Still, it's only a stupid key.' Sam stood up and left the room in a hurry. I was left in the brooding silence of the living room. The light was dimming as evening turned slowly to night. Through my window, I could see Tammy making her way slowly up our drive, stopping now and then to sit down and look around in that strange way that cats have. I knew that shortly, I would hear the cat flap open and close, and she would appear silently beside me like some messenger from another world.

I wondered what was going on with Sam that had suddenly precipitated this turn in favour of Nick. Maybe it had been percolating away for ages without my realizing. It seemed to be landing on the heels of a few other things, though, with Steve causing so much trouble, Cathy kicking up about her involvement with Steve, and now Nick claiming some sort of rights to share the house. I felt like my life was being funnelled down a narrow tunnel towards an end that I couldn't quite figure out, but it didn't feel good.

9

At work I managed to contact a good embassy person who was very proactive in helping repatriate that underage girl who had been sent over to get married, so that felt like something of a victory. Finishing early, I went for coffee with one of my colleagues and shot the breeze in a carefree way that reminded me that life was still going on out there, and maybe I shouldn't get so worked up about my domestic situation. Resolving to apply that feeling to my life, I poached a nice, long fillet of hake, threw on some green beans and potatoes, and cracked open a bottle of red that had been eyeballing me from the wine rack for a couple of weeks. It had been on special offer at the local off-licence from my favourite French wine region, the Languedoc, and I had resolved to keep it for a special occasion. Reclaiming my former carefree attitude felt very like a special occasion to me.

The first bump in that new, carefree road came when Nick appeared at the door. He didn't have to say anything. I'd had the key cut earlier in the day and handed it to him without inviting him in.

'So you'll just be using this now and then and only to keep tools out the back or to make yourself a quick cuppa.'

'Oh, what are they? The Ts and Cs?' Nick smiled at his own joke.

'If you like. I think it's good to be clear, don't you?'

'Sure, but we're not business partners, are we?'

'No? What are we, then?' That slipped out before I could stop it, but Nick had an uncanny ability to get right under my skin.

Nick hesitated. The smile had disappeared. He played with the key in his hand. 'As Sam said, it's just a key.'

'And that's exactly the way I want to leave it. It's just a key and should only be used when necessary.'

'All right, all right, don't get your knickers in a twist. You can have it back if it's such a big deal.' Nick stretched the hand with the key towards me. I actually felt like crying with frustration. The glass of Languedoc was a million miles away.

'No, it's okay. We made an agreement, and I'll stick to it. Now, I have food on the table.' With that, I closed the door as gently as I could. Nick stayed where he was on the doorstep, the key still in his outstretched hand.

Determined to put that behind me, I stuck my laptop on the table and scrolled through Facebook as I ate, indulging myself in peeking into the carefully curated online lives of those I knew. I marvelled at other families and their apparent cohesion and the joy they shared in making quirky muffins or gingerbread men and the family events that produced such unbridled merriment. I had more or less given up posting after the split with Nick. I knew my kids wouldn't be seen dead around my Facebook page, so it wasn't like they'd feel left out or anything. I felt the wine slip into a place that needed some serious TLC and thought that maybe my plan for the new carefree life was going to work out after all.

Cathy put a nice dampener on that by arriving back with

the news that she was babysitting at Steve's. She dropped it casually as she helped herself to some of the haddock and veg. Her back was turned to me at the time. I had just been considering offering her some of the precious wine, but that urge dried up pretty quickly.

What was I to say? You can't go babysitting because he's a criminal and you are not savvy enough to be in any way involved with someone like that? I knew Cathy well enough that she would counter any argument I would put to her.

'Well, don't be late. You have college in the morning, don't you?' That was as neutral an input as I could come up with.

'He's just going to the gym, so it shouldn't be a late one.' Cathy delivered this in a casual tone, like it was something we discussed every day.

'And remember what I talked to you about. You need to be careful.' My protective maternal side couldn't resist coming out with that, but as soon as I'd said it, I regretted it.

Cathy glowered at me through the steam rising from dinner. 'I told you, Mam, I can look after myself.'

'I know you can, but it's always useful to have another perspective on things.'

'It's an annoying perspective, and I don't need it, thank you very much.' Cathy took her phone out and started scrolling through it. Normally, I don't allow phones at the dinner table, but here I was with Facebook open in front of me, so I had lost the moral high ground.

There was nothing more I could say that wouldn't be met with open hostility, so I just let the moment play out, but I couldn't help thinking it was like watching a car crash in slow motion. Steve was bad news. Of that I had no doubt.

I did my best to enjoy another glass of the Languedoc once Cathy had left. Sam showed his face briefly to announce he was heading over to Philly's. They didn't seem like such a bad crowd over there, lots of music and lads going in with slabs of beer, but nothing out of the ordinary for student life. I had seen McCann go in and out of the place, but as Philly was his nephew, that was no great surprise.

Tammy kept me company for most of the glass of wine. She purred quietly and only moved to do that weird clawing thing they do every now and again. It's like they're building up to doing a great leap off the chair, but they just sit back down again. I was grateful for the mysterious company of a creature that was generally issue-free and definitely nonhuman. She did drop suddenly off the chair, though, after a while, and I heard the cat flap at the front door open and shut.

I took that as a cue to bundle myself off to bed, allowing myself a slow, easy ascent, taking all the accoutrements I'd need like phone, radio, book. I had a bath with scented candles and massaged a good dollop of moisturizer in. Looking at myself in the mirror in the candlelight, I felt the image that faced me wasn't too bad. I had kept more or less the shape I'd had since my late teens, on the thinner side of chunky. *If I were a wine*, I thought, *I'd be described as full-bodied, mature, with lots of different flavours waiting to be explored.*

I took to the fresh, clean sheets of my bed with gusto and flicked on to some chat show on the radio where people vent about all the things that people seem to want to vent about, but it made for easy listening. The host did a good job of egging them on, and the overall result was trashy but entertaining, which was exactly what I was looking for.

I must have slid into a gentle sleep because the radio was still on when I was roused from my slumber by a loud knocking on the front door. I had incorporated the knocking into whatever dream I was having, so it took me a good minute to compute that real life was actually impinging on my night's sleep.

I went groggily out onto the landing. The knocking continued. I assumed it was Sam or Cathy who had forgotten their key. I checked my watch and saw it was two a.m. Cathy's door was open, so she wasn't in yet. Sam's was open too. As I went down the stairs, I could smell something. At first, I wasn't sure what it was, but as I got lower, I could make out the acrid smell of smoke. Once in the hall, I could see the silhouette of whoever was knocking, and behind them, I saw the unmistakable orange and red flashes of a flame.

Oh, my God, there's a fire, I thought. My first reaction was that it could be my car, but the flames seemed to be a little more distant. I rushed and pulled the door open. Outside was a breathless, red-faced Paul, pointing back towards the end of my drive. There, right beside my car, was a rubbish bin that I had put out earlier for collection the next morning. It was billowing with thick, choking, acrid smoke, and through the smoke were dancing tongues of flame. The smell and the heat were overwhelming.

'I've called the fire brigade,' Paul panted. Even as he said it, I could hear a siren wailing closer, and within what seemed only seconds, a fire truck pulled into our estate. The firemen jumped from their truck and ushered me and Paul back before uncoiling the hose and spraying the bin with a powerful jet of water. The effect of the water was to send a massive plume of steamy smoke billowing into the air. The flames quickly disappeared, but the cloud of steamy smoke hung thick and defiant in the night air.

'You had a close one there,' one of the firemen said. 'Another minute and your car would have gone up too.'

I looked at my car and could see a little black shading on the bonnet where the smoke had scorched it.

Cathy came hurrying out of Steve's house. Steve followed after her.

'Are you okay, Mam?' she asked me, putting an arm around my shoulder.

'I'm grand, love, thanks.'

'Some little thugs must have done that,' Steve said, nodding towards the bin.

Fred came out to join us. He was in slippers and pyjamas. 'I heard all the commotion. Who the hell would do something like that?'

'You never know,' Steve said, looking over the estate. 'It could be just somebody who wandered in, looking to do some mischief.'

'Or it could be somebody from the estate,' Fred said quickly.

'Well, who in this nice, quiet estate would do a thing like that?' Steve asked.

'It doesn't matter,' Cathy said, grabbing my arm and starting to lead me towards the house. 'The main thing is that everyone is okay, and no serious damage was done.'

I hesitated before going in. I didn't like the idea of leaving Fred and Steve outside together.

'Thanks for coming out. I think we all need to put it behind us now.'

They both looked at me. Fred hesitated before turning back up his drive and into his house. Steve waited even longer. He waved at Cathy.

'Sleep tight,' he said with a smile.

I lay awake in bed for what felt like hours. I heard Sam come in at some stage and was at least grateful that we were all safe under the one roof. It was deeply troubling to think that someone might set fire to our bin. I ran through various possibilities at how it might have happened. Now that Sam seemed to be smoking weed, had he put a butt in the bin hours earlier, and maybe it took that long to actually produce a fire?

I couldn't recall putting anything in myself that would generate a flame. If it wasn't Sam, then the only other option was a malicious act. Unfortunately, that seemed like the most likely scenario, so I was left wondering who would do something like that, and again unfortunately, the most likely candidate seemed to be Steve. That exchange we'd had the other night was far from pleasant. In fact, it would probably be described as slightly menacing. He had been implying that I was alone and vulnerable and that he had both Cathy and Nick onside with him. He had been out at the gym, so he could have had the chance to do something just after he got back and before he went in to Cathy. The big question, though, was why he would do something like that if it was him? What was he trying to achieve? Was Cathy part of his scheme, if there even was a scheme? I fell into a troubled sleep that was all too short and woke feeling frazzled and exhausted in the morning.

10

I found it very hard to concentrate on work, which is not what you want when you are dealing with people in a heightened state of distress. There was another young girl who needed emergency placement. She had been self-harming at home. Her mum was a single parent and had to go to work, and she was afraid what her daughter might do in her absence, so we agreed that a temporary stay in emergency accommodation with a structured regime and counselling would be the best solution for the moment. I spent the day putting all the supports in place, but inevitably, there was a lot of waiting around, and while I was waiting, I couldn't help but think about my own situation.

If Steve had an agenda, which he appeared to have, what result was he looking for, and how far would he go to achieve it? If he had set my bin on fire and I was a target, then what would be next? Most of all, I worried about Cathy's safety. If he was prepared to conduct a vendetta against me for whatever reason, then what were his plans for Cathy? I was beginning to wonder if I should, after all, have considered the offer that strange couple made on the house. I hadn't entertained them or even gone as far as to see if they were bona fide. Maybe I should have, and I could have made a quick sale with no estate agents involved.

But then I checked myself. What was I thinking? That was my home, and I couldn't let a few bad experiences put me off staying there. Steve would probably move on eventually, and things would return to normal. Hopefully, Cathy would see sense too and see Steve for who he really was.

That evening after dinner, I was sitting in the living room, having a mug of tea and looking out at the street when I heard music blaring from Steve's. Looking around to his side, I saw him working on yet another car, door open and music coming from the stereo. I felt it was a good opportunity to feel him out about the previous night's events, so I steeled myself and went over to his drive.

He looked nonchalantly up as I approached, and wiped his hands with a rag he was holding. He made no effort to turn the music down, so I gestured towards the car and did a mime of turning a dial down with my hand. He smiled but didn't move for a few seconds before leaning in and turning it down a couple of notches.

'Could I have a word?' I half-shouted up the drive. I didn't want to venture in, as then I'd be on his property.

'Sure.' He continued wiping his hands and walked slowly towards me. A defiant smile was spread across his face.

'It's about last night. You were up late. I wondered if you saw anything.'

'Nope. I was busy.'

I didn't like what he was trying to imply, but I ignored it. I had come for a purpose and was determined to see it through.

'Cathy was out pretty quickly, so you must have seen what was going on. Hard to miss it, really, but I was more interested in whether you'd seen anyone dodgy around earlier.'

'Dodgy?' His smile became even broader. 'Now what would dodgy people be doing around a nice area like this?'

'You know what I mean. Did you see any teenagers out or anything unusual?'

'No, nothing unusual. Cathy and I were having a little chat. Those chats can be quite distracting.'

'I wonder who would do a thing like that, then, setting fire to a bin, nearly setting fire to a car in the process.'

'You'd wonder, all right. Maybe it was an accident. Accidents happen. All sorts of accidents happen. People make wrong decisions. Half the time, they don't know they're making wrong decisions, and that's when the accidents happen. Take your eye off the ball, and *boom*.'

'So you didn't see anything?' I could see I wasn't getting anywhere. He was just using the opportunity to goad me, if anything. I wasn't quite sure what he was trying to say, but I didn't like it.

'You seem like a smart woman.' The smile had disappeared from his face. 'I told you once. I don't like having to repeat myself, but no, I didn't see anything.'

Just then, I heard the familiar sound of Nick's pickup rattling down the road. I turned to see him pull up in front of Philly's house. McCann pulled up behind him in his Merc and jumped out energetically. I took the chance to walk away from Steve and over towards them. Nick climbed out of the pickup and gave me a businesslike nod of the head before turning to McCann.

'Hi, June, how are we? Sorry to hear about the bin,' McCann said.

Nick looked confused; then he saw the blackened top of the bin on the other side of my front wall.

'Oh, God,' he said. 'That looks nasty.'

'It was. I could have lost the car and all.'

'Any idea how it happened?'

'That's the million-dollar question, and the answer is no.' I looked at McCann and thought I saw him throw a glance in Steve's direction. I followed his gaze, but Steve was just back working on the car, music thumping out.

'It's one of those things that can happen,' he said, looking back at me. 'Unpleasant and definitely something to give you a bit of a fright. I've seen it, though, in some of my properties over the years. Tenants can be careless or even not realise that some of the stuff they throw in the bin is combustible. I'm not saying you put anything in, but you have kids, and there can even be people passing in the street. Once the bins are out for collection, you just never know.' He looked back over at Steve. 'I'd better go over and tell our friend to turn the music down. It's a bit late in the day for that.'

McCann gave me a broad smile and headed over to Steve. A few seconds later, the music was turned right down, but Steve gave a long look over in my direction before he returned to working on his car.

'I'm just going to leave some of this stuff in the back as we agreed,' Nick said, gesturing towards some of the tools in the pickup. He didn't wait for a response but started dragging things out and bringing them in through the front door, which was still open.

I went back inside, and after moving the tools in, I saw Nick hesitate in the kitchen area. He looked like he might go for the kettle and make himself some tea.

'It's getting late,' I said. 'I'm just going to flake out now. I had a hard day, and I had to have yet another chat with that guy Steve. He was playing that music very loudly.'

'Oh, that's a nuisance,' Nick said without much conviction.

'It is, and I'm afraid of what Fred next door will do because I can see he's getting really riled by the whole thing.

Paul too. He's not the most stable, and Steve has already hit him.'

'Yeah, Steve told me about that. He said Paul went for him.'

'I don't think there's any comparison between a tough, young guy like Steve and a middle-aged alcoholic. Steve could have easily got rid of Paul without thumping him.'

'Still. You can't blame him.'

I could feel irritation rising fast. Nick seemed to be taking Steve's side, ignoring the fact that this was an upset to me too. I didn't have the will or the energy to have it out with him. I'd got used to Nick's selfish perspective on life, and frankly, I'd had enough of it.

'As I said, I'm just going to relax now. Didn't get much sleep with the bin thing last night.' I actually closed my eyes to reinforce my need. I heard him shuffle off, and the front door mercifully closed.

That night, I fell into bed at ten thirty. I didn't even have the energy for a pampering bath, just grabbed my book and must have fallen asleep within a couple of pages.

I woke in a state of confusion. There was a loud, persistent noise, and I hadn't a clue what it was. I opened my eyes and sat up. It was coming from outside, but it was close. I struggled out of bed, and as I hit the landing, I started to recognize the constant beeping sound of a car alarm.

Nervously, I pulled the front door open and peered out into the darkness. The sound was coming from my car, and my side lights were flashing in unison with the beeping. I grabbed for my keys, which were hanging in the hallway, clicked the open button and then the lock button, and the alarm went silent. Peering around the drive, I checked for anything unusual but saw nothing. Now the alarm had gone off, there was just an eerie silence. I walked tentatively towards my car. The doors were locked now, so if there had been anyone inside, they were now locked in. Reaching back into the hall, I switched on the porch light, and that made the car and its contents clearly visible. There was nobody inside and no damage to the outside that I could see.

So what triggered the alarm? I wondered.

Walking around the car, less nervous now, I inspected it. Anecdotally, I had heard that a bird flying against a window or some small impact could trigger an alarm, but what sort of birds flew at night? It could have been a bat, I supposed, but that would need to be a pretty big bat.

Seeing nothing on the driver's side, I walked around, checking the passenger doors and windows, and that was where I got my answer. The front passenger window was down about an inch.

That's funny, I thought. *If I'm putting a window down for air, it's always the driver's side.* I hadn't given anyone a lift, so it was strange that one was down unless I had lowered it, thinking it was the driver's side, and then forgotten all about it. *Still,* I wondered, *would that trigger an alarm, and why would it be so delayed?* It was hours since I had parked.

The only other option I could think of was that someone had tried to force the window to try to get into the car or that they had just forced the window to set off the alarm. I looked around, fear taking hold again. If someone had done that, then they had done it recently. They could still be in the vicinity. In fact, they could be somewhere very close, watching me. I steeled myself, acting as casually as I could, and opened the car again. Sitting in, I turned on the ignition enough to close the passenger window. My heart was thumping and my hands shaking, but I continued to move slowly. Locking the car again, I went back into the house and felt a flood of relief as I closed the door behind me.

Once inside, I turned the kitchen light on and got myself a glass of water. I checked that the living room blinds were fully closed. The sense that someone might be watching me had followed me right inside. Sitting at the table, I felt my hand shake as I sipped at the water. The liquid was cool and helped to ground me again.

If it was no accident and I hadn't left the window open, and that seemed like the most likely scenario, then who had forced it down and why? The immediate answer that came to me was that someone with a knowledge of cars would be most likely to do something like that, someone who knew just what they had to do to set off a car alarm without actually breaking anything. I thought back to the way that Steve had seemed to be glaring at me after McCann asked him to turn the music down, and I felt I didn't have to look much further for an answer.

11

The next day was a Saturday, and I was able to have a lie-in. I was dead to the world till about eleven when I woke to the sound of someone downstairs. I presumed it was Sam or Cathy, although they were usually late risers at the weekend.

Must have some college work to catch up on, I thought.

Then I heard whistling, which would have been totally uncharacteristic for either of them. I sat bolt upright in the bed. I could feel my muscles stiffen with tension. Creeping out of bed, I put a dressing gown on and slipped quietly onto the landing. The whistling continued. The kettle was boiling, and then I heard a dry cough that I recognized as one that Nick occasionally came out with.

What the hell is he doing here without telling me on a Saturday morning?

He was sitting at the dining table when I came down, a mug of tea steaming in front of him and a packet of biscuits open.

'Morning,' he said cheerily as I appeared.

Initially, I thought I'd be as circumspect as I could, but that went out the window with his bluff cheeriness.

'How come you're here?'

'Oh, had to get going on those hedges McCann was talking about, and I've some other work lined up early in the week, so no time like the present.' He snapped a biscuit in half and dunked it.

'But it's Saturday. And it's early.'

'I know. I wasn't too popular back at the home base taking off like that, but there's a lot of work in it, so I had to get a start.'

I sat down and ran my hands through my hair. 'Nick, when I gave you keys, it wasn't like a carte blanche to let yourself in whenever you want. I thought it would be just during the week when I wasn't here. I've had a very stressful week. The weekend is my downtime.'

'God, I know it must have been stressful with the bin and everything, but hopefully that'll be the end of it.'

'I don't think you're getting the point here. I would prefer if you didn't call unannounced on a weekend morning is what I mean.'

'Oh.' He paused midway into sipping from his hot tea.

'Yeah. That's it, Nick, in black and white. I don't want you to be taking advantage of the access.'

'It's funny you should say that.' He returned to sipping his tea. 'We're having a bit of difficulty with our own place. The lease is up soon, and the landlord wants to sell up, so we'll have to move out.'

'Sorry to hear that, but how does that relate?'

'Well, we might think about buying our own place.'

'That's nice.' I still didn't see what the connection to our current impasse was.

'And a little birdy told me that someone had made an offer on this house.'

'A little birdy? Who said that?'

'I don't want to be telling tales, but someone told me there was a couple looking for property around here, and they had made both you and Fred an offer.'

'Maybe they did, but I have no intention of moving.'

'Well, let's not forget there's two of us in this. My name is still on the deeds of the house.'

'But we have an agreement that this will stay as the family home.'

'Yes, but if it came to a situation where I was going to be homeless, then I think you would be obliged to sell if you got a good enough offer.'

I was shocked by what Nick was saying. He seemed to be dragging me into his own housing difficulties. If I didn't play ball, how far would he go? 'Are you threatening to get legal about this?'

'That's not what I'm saying, but I would like to be kept in the loop. You never told me an offer was made.'

'I didn't tell you because I have no intention of selling. This is my and your kids' family home. The circumstances that led to your moving out are your responsibility.'

'Maybe so, but we will have to see this as an evolving situation. All parties involved need to be taken into consideration. Now, I'd better get down to cutting those hedges.'

He rinsed his mug, left it on the draining board, and marched out. I wondered how he had got wind of the offer on the house. Maybe Fred had said it to someone who passed it on to someone else. Still, I really didn't like the language Nick was using. There was a quasi-legal aspect to it, like he had been talking to someone about his rights. The way he was suddenly being proprietorial and assertive was troubling me also. If he was on the verge of losing the place he was currently living in, it would only get worse.

I needed to unwind after that, so I went back to bed and

read for a while, took a long, hot shower, had a lazy brunch, and went around to the local salon to get my nails done. I picked up some pizza bases and salad mix at the supermarket with a nice bottle of red. I was determined to continue my lazy day. The kids were always happy to see pizza on the table.

Once I got back home, I saw Nick's pickup was gone and noted that he had indeed scalped a lot of the hedge around Philly's house. *Maybe I was being a bit harsh on him for having tea in the kitchen*, I thought. He was, after all, doing work that would bring in much-needed maintenance money at the end of the month. But then I remembered his spiel about the house and what could be seen as threatening pre-emptive moves towards getting me to sell up. The feelings of sympathy for him quickly dried up again.

After lounging around with my laptop and seeing that the day was pleasant, I stuck on some gardening gloves and went out to tend my jasmine, which I had noticed was starting to spill all over the place. It needed a bit of trimming.

I was snipping delicately at it when I noticed McCann's Merc pulling up outside Philly's house. He jumped out and gave the hedging a cursory look-over; then he spotted me in the garden and walked briskly over.

'How are we?' he asked with a warm smile. 'Hope things have settled down a bit.'

'Well, a little. My car alarm went off last night. Not sure what it was, but it's always a bit of a worry.'

He looked around the estate as if looking for a culprit. 'You never know, do you? Nine times out of ten, it's just the wind or something knocking off it, but you're left with that feeling that it could be something more.'

I didn't bother to go into details about the window. 'Yes, with everything else that's been going on, it was unsettling.'

He nodded his head in emphatic agreement. 'I know exactly what you mean.'

I wasn't sure if he did know, but he did a good job of looking sincere. *Quite the salesman,* I thought. *Plenty of charm.* Which, I had to admit, I didn't object to. I'd had enough of harsh reality during the week and welcomed a bit of escapism.

'I hope you don't mind me saying so, but I have a lot of admiration for someone like you, a single parent who has to keep the whole show on the road. It can't be easy.'

'It has its moments, all right,' I conceded.

'I know Nick is there to give a helping hand, but it can't be easy steering two young people through their teens these days.'

'Nick?' I said with probably too much of a dose of incredulity because he laughed.

'I'm sure he does his best.'

Just then, Fred came back from a walk. He was about to continue up his drive when he turned and came over.

'I was just admiring June's garden,' McCann said with an affable smile.

'Yes, we keep our gardens well around here. Most of us take pride in our houses.' Here he looked deliberately in the direction of Steve's house.

'I know, but people need a chance too.'

'I wonder how many chances they need. Some people don't want to listen. They don't want to learn.'

McCann nodded as if in agreement, but I could see a frown spreading across his forehead.

'I've spoken to Mr Murray, as you know.'

'For all the good it did.'

'We do our best.'

'Well, *we* do, anyway. You know what? This is quickly becoming a police matter is what I think.'

McCann sighed and walked over to Philly's.

I stayed outside and got back to trimming the jasmine and then the sweet pea. Fred stayed where he was, looking agitated. I was hoping he'd cool down if I left him to his own devices for a couple of minutes, but I was wrong.

'I don't buy what that guy McCann is saying at all. He hasn't lifted a finger in terms of our main problem here.' He nodded his head in the direction of Steve's. 'McCann is nothing but a smooth talker. I don't trust him at all, and I'm coming to the end of my tether with the situation next door. Between the cars and the dogs and the music, I'm going to put a complaint in to the police and let them handle it.'

'I'm not sure the police can do anything much about it. They can call down and advise, but unless he's actually breaking the law, what can they do?'

'I don't care. It's time someone stood up to this new crowd. I'm sure we can get something the police can act on.' With that, he stormed back off to his house. I felt so sorry for him, an old man on his own whose tranquil retirement had been turned upside down, but at the same time, I was concerned. Things were bad, but we didn't want an out-and-out battle on our hands.

I didn't hear from Fred again until late on Sunday evening when I heard my phone ping and saw that I had a text from him.

June. We need to talk. I have some very important infor-
mation regarding what's going on in our estate.

That was short and cryptic. Fred almost never texted me unless it was something urgent. This was obviously urgent, but it was late, so it would have to wait till the next day.

12

That day at work, I kept thinking about the text Fred had sent me. What kind of information could he have uncovered? I tried calling him at one stage, but he didn't pick up, so I left it. Maybe he didn't want to discuss whatever it was over the phone. Chances were, he didn't have his phone nearby anyway. Fred was of an age where the phone was a distant appendage, not glued to his person at all times like the younger generation.

I arrived home at six and defrosted a chicken curry I'd cooked weeks ago. There was just enough there for the three of us at a stretch. Putting on some basmati to go with it, I waited till the rice boiled, then turned the heat right down to let the water soak fully into the rice and leave it nice and fluffy. Having done that, I ran over to Fred's and knocked on the door. There was no answer, which was odd, because his car was there, but he could have gone for one of his long walks. I texted him to let him know I'd called in and he could pop into me when he was back.

I thought about Fred as I tucked into the curry. He had been at a loss since his wife, Margaret, died a few years ago.

They'd been so close and had great plans for their retirement together. Both had worked in the Public Service. She had been in the Department of Health and he in Roads and Transport. Their schedules and their lives were closely interwoven, so much so that they had retired at the same time, even though Fred was a bit older. They'd wanted to travel to Europe together, maybe even get a villa somewhere hot and spend the winters there. Then Margaret got a diagnosis of breast cancer, and their world fell apart. Fred changed overnight from someone who was enjoying the fruits of life to someone who was worried and overwrought. Margaret took it more in her stride. She got chemo and got the all-clear. Fred bounced back into life again, but the cancer came back, more malevolent this time, and Margaret was given a matter of months to live. At the time, I was going through my own difficulties with Nick, so I wasn't there for Fred as much as I would have liked. She died shortly after, and Fred just went right into himself. I called in as much as I could, making excuses to do so, like bringing in freshly baked bread or muffins or even ready-made meals that I pretended to have too much of and said I was afraid they would go off if someone didn't eat them.

His house was like a shrine to their time together. The mantelpiece and wall in his living room were covered with photographs of their life together, all the places that they had visited, everything from their wedding day right up to the last years. They had just one son, Cathal, who had gone to work as an engineer in Canada. He was back for a couple of weeks around the funeral but had to go back again. Since then, it was just Fred, alone and now disturbed and frustrated by the way our street had changed. I felt the same way, nervous even, with the two incidents during the week, but I was determined to try to keep a cool head and not get drawn into a fight I couldn't handle.

Sam came shuffling in about seven, and I dished him up some curry.

'Good day at college?'

'Not bad. They're getting on my case about assignments, though. There's too many all at once.'

'Take them one by one and ask for an extension if you need it.'

'They won't give me any more extensions.'

'Oh, so you had some already?'

'Maybe. It's still too much.'

I thought about Sam's state in recent times and how he seemed to be stoned half the time.

'Maybe you should give the socializing a break for a while and just knuckle down so you get all that out of the way; then you can go back to socializing.'

'What, and, like, give up my life? No way. I'm a young person, remember. I've got a life to live.'

I didn't like the implications of that, but I said nothing. It was like he thought I had no life to live, ignoring the fact that I spent most of my time keeping the whole shooting show on the road. I didn't feel like taking him on. There were bigger fish to fry. I was starting to worry about Fred. Surely, he would have called in to me by now.

'Were you around today?' I asked Sam, and he glowered in hostility at me like it was a leading question.

'No, actually, I was in college.'

'I'm only asking to see if you saw Fred.'

'No, I hardly ever see him, anyway. He's, like, a total recluse.' Sam cleared his plate and shuffled off upstairs.

I watched news for half an hour, checking my phone repeatedly for a reply from Fred, but there was none. I waited another half hour, checking out the window every now and then to see if I could see him walking back into the estate, but I saw no sign of him, so I called back into his house. *Maybe he is having a nap upstairs,* I thought, and knocked a little harder on the door, but I still got no reply. *Where the hell could he be?* I peered in the windows but couldn't see very far in. I tried knocking on the windows then and listened carefully for any response.

Was that some sort of sound I heard from inside? I wasn't sure, but it sounded like something moving or a very faint voice. *Maybe he's had a fall,* I thought. I had a spare key to his house, as we had swapped keys with each other years ago in case we locked ourselves out. I was reluctant to use it in case he was still out of the house. It wouldn't do for him to come back and find me inside, but I was getting genuinely worried, so I had to do something.

I got the key and put it in his door. My hand shook as I turned it. The door opened easily, and I was straight into his hallway. Stopping to listen again, I thought I detected the sound of some sort of movement coming from inside.

'Fred?' I called and heard my voice echo back. No answer, so I took a couple more steps inside. He had a kitchen-cum-living room like myself, so his living room was through a set of double doors to my left. One of those doors was already open, so I stepped through. He had a long table just like I had, and then behind that were a couple of armchairs and an open fire. Over the mantelpiece, I could see all the photos of Fred and Margaret at various stages of their lives. Having been in Fred's house before, I knew he kept it neat and tidy, but the scene in front of me was anything but. The living room was a complete mess with everything thrown around the place, cushions ripped open, their stuffing spilling all over the floor, the sofa upended. Something terrible had happened here. Someone had flashed like a whirlwind through Fred's living room. But where was he?

'Fred?' I called again. I was thinking of turning around and leaving, afraid that whoever had done this might still be in the house, when I heard a noise. I couldn't quite make it out, but it was coming from the other end of the long table. Butterflies started racing around my stomach as I walked slowly around. There was definitely a faint sound coming from that direction. Slowly, tentatively, I came around the side of the table so I had a view of the floor on the other side. The first thing I saw was a dark stain that had spread across the varnished floorboards that ran under his table. The stain was narrow at the top and became wider as I approached. My whole body was starting to tremble in anticipation of what I might find. There, at the widest part of the dark stain, I could see something solid, white in places but with garish patches of red, purple, and blue.

My recollection from that point became hazy, but I remember stopping and going into a spasm of shaking before letting out a scream, then bending down over the prostrate body and crushed skull of Fred, who lay curled up and stiff, covered in dried blood, his skin a sickly yellow colour. Leaning down, I touched his hand. It felt cold and waxy, but there was still a flicker of warmth there. Then I saw his arm move. It could have been a spasm or could have slid after I touched his hand. I jumped back and screamed again.

Gathering myself, I leaned in again and whispered, 'Fred.'

He was completely still again. The caked blood that covered him made it hard to see his face. Then, as I started to pull away, I heard a sound coming from his mouth. It came again. The same sound. His lips were barely moving, but it was like he was trying to speak.

'What is it, Fred?' I asked, hoping that if I engaged him, it might bring him back to consciousness.

He tried speaking again, but it was just coming in a whisper. He was making what seemed like *B* sounds, but I wasn't sure if it was just the effort of trying to talk, but there it was again, some word with a *B* at the beginning and in the middle. I could see the effort of speaking was too much for him, so I touched him on the shoulder and said, 'It's okay, Fred. It's okay. I can hear you. I'm going to get help now.'

I rushed from the house and back into my living room to grab my mobile and called emergency services.

'I need an ambulance. Fast. There's someone dying. And police. Something terrible has happened,' I spluttered when they answered. My heart was racing, and the hand that held the phone was shaking uncontrollably.

13

The next few minutes went by in a blur. The emergency services kept me on the line, asking about the condition of the person, making sure they had the right address, and they only hung up when I could see the ambulance and the Garda car turn into our street. The ambulance pulled up abruptly, and a man and woman jumped out. They were quickly followed by two Gardai, who pulled up behind them and approached me.

'Was it you who made the call?' one of them asked.

'Yes, June Sweeney is my name. I'm his neighbour.'

'And the man in question is?'

'Fred Summers.'

'Is he inside the property?'

'Yes, he's on the floor behind a table. He's dying.'

The Gardai and the ambulance crew hurried through Fred's door. I went in after them, but one of the Gardai gestured for me to stay back. I could see the paramedics leaning over him and talking quietly to each other. The female paramedic crouched down beside Fred and stayed there for a minute. I couldn't see what she was doing because the table blocked my view, but when she stood again, she shook her head both to her co-worker and to the Gardai. There was a brief, hushed discussion between the paramedics and the Gardai before all four left the room together. One of the Gardai stopped at Fred's double doors and pulled a piece of yellow tape from one side of the door to the other. He looked at me.

'It looks like your neighbour was assaulted. I'm afraid he has died from his injuries. This house will now be designated a crime scene, so we'll have to ask you to leave. My colleague will take a brief statement from you, if that's all right.'

'Of course,' I replied, but my mind was a million miles away. I was desperately trying to compute what had just happened. As I tried to gather my thoughts outside, I saw Steve come out of his house to survey the scene. He frowned and looked agitated. At the same time, Cathy came down the street. I could see her checking her phone as she walked, but then she looked up and saw the Garda car and the ambulance and me. Her mouth dropped open, and she hurried across.

'What happened, Mam?' She had grabbed a hold of my arm. At the same time, Steve walked over to the two of us.

'It's Fred. They think he was assaulted. He's dead.'

Cathy went pale and lifted her hand to her mouth. Steve shook his head.

'What do they think happened?' he asked.

I was too numb to answer, so I just shook my head.

Steve answered his own question. 'It's too early to say, I suppose.'

'Oh, my God. That is so awful,' Cathy said. 'The poor guy. Oh, my God,' she repeated.

The second Garda beckoned me over towards their car at that point. He had a notebook out. He was tall, sallow skinned, and spoke slowly.

'June Sweeney, am I correct?'

'Yes.'

'And it was you who put in the emergency call.'

'That's right.'

'Could you describe briefly the circumstances leading up to the discovery and also what you saw when you got inside?'

I set about describing just what had happened on the day, but I did mention that I had got a text from Fred to say he had something important to tell me the day before.

'Do you have any idea what he wanted to talk to you about?'

I looked over at Steve. He and Cathy were talking, looking towards Fred's house.

'I'm not sure, but things have changed on our street recently. We've had some new people move in, and Fred wasn't too happy about the way things had changed.'

The Garda paused and looked at me. 'Was there any incident in particular that had bothered him?'

Again, I looked over at Steve. He seemed to be out of hearing range, but I wasn't taking any chances.

'Just the nuisance, some cars were badly parked, and a bit of extra noise.'

'He was an elderly man,' the Garda said ambivalently.

'Yes, he was, but I shared his discomfort at what was happening.'

'You did?' the Garda left that as an open-ended question.

'Well, yes, it has been disturbing at times.'

He closed his notebook. 'Okay, June, thanks for your time. We'll be back in touch, I'm sure. This will most likely turn into a criminal investigation, so we'll probably be looking for witnesses and information.'

He reached into his car and got on his radio. Meanwhile, the other Garda had taken up a position at the front door of Fred's house. The whole scene was so surreal. I didn't know what to do. Cathy came over to me and put an arm around my shoulder.

'You should probably get back into the house and get a cup of tea.'

I followed her meekly into our house and sat at the table. Cathy presented me with a mug of tea, and I sipped distractedly from it. I felt shivery all of a sudden and could feel myself shake. The hot tea helped keep the shivers in check. It was impossible to process what I had just seen and been through.

Cathy sat beside me.

'That must have been awful, walking in on Fred like that.'

'He had texted me. There was something he wanted to tell me.'

Cathy sat back. 'What do you think it could have been?'

'I don't know, but it must have been something to do with what's been going on in the street is my only guess.'

'But what could he have discovered that was so urgent?'

'I really don't know.'

That was the truth. In the little time I'd had to think about it, I couldn't figure out what would have been so urgent that he needed to talk to me and that it needed to be on our own. It must have been something significant, but I was left wondering what it was.

That night, more Garda cars arrived, and detectives in white body suits worked busily both inside the house and out in the garden. They had strong lights shining, so it looked like a movie set. I looked out every now and then and watched the eerie scene unfold. It was like the street was no longer ours. Cathy stayed with me until it was time for bed. I really didn't know what to do with myself. Then, to reinforce the whole thing, I heard something on the news about a man being found dead and the police looking into it, but it was too early to say the exact cause of death.

The word *death* followed me when I went to bed. *What has happened to our street? Who is doing this? Is it connected to the bin and the car alarm?*

I had no answers. The thoughts just kept swirling round and round my head. At one stage, I went to the bathroom, and I could still see the glow of the lights outside.

In the morning, I called in sick to work. I didn't have it in me to explain what had happened. Everyone would know soon enough if, as the Gardai had said, he had been assaulted and killed.

A short time later, two athletic-looking men in sports jackets knocked on the door. They flashed badges as I opened it.

'Detective Mooney and Detective Sullivan,' the one holding the 'Sullivan' badge said. 'June Sweeney, is that right?'

'Yes.' I felt both nervous and reassured to have them standing there.

'As you were the person who put in the call to emergency services, we'd like to go through the order of events,' he continued.

'Of course. Come in.' I didn't like the idea of talking to them in full view.

They slowly followed me in. I gestured to two chairs, and they sat down, looking around the room as they did.

'Tea?'

'Lovely,' Mooney said with a smile.

Once we were all seated with mugs of tea, Sullivan got going. Mooney seemed to be there to observe.

'So, June, would you like to run us through the incident to the best of your recollection? Don't forget, every detail may be important no matter how trivial it seems.'

I shakily recounted all that I could of the day before and

put in a little about the difficulties we had been having, including my bin going on fire and the car alarm going off.

Sullivan listened carefully. Mooney took some notes. They were both attentive, considerate men in their late thirties.

'It looks like your neighbour was assaulted,' Sullivan said. 'He probably suffered blunt force trauma that led to his death. We haven't recovered a murder weapon yet, but we are searching the area. The pathologist is due later today, and he will give us conclusive analysis of the cause of death. Our initial investigation leads us to believe that the perpetrator may have been in some way known to the victim or may have surprised the victim and forced entry to his house. They may have been looking for something in the house, or they may have sought to rob something from the property, we can't be sure. Do you know of anyone who had a grudge against Mr Summers?'

'Well, we have had an ongoing dispute with Fred's immediate neighbour, Steve Murray, but it wasn't that serious. There was a brief altercation between Mr Murray and another neighbour over noise.'

'But not with Mr Summers?'

I shook my head.

'Sometimes, it's hard to judge how seriously people take these disputes. Anything else we should know about?'

'Not that I'm aware of. Fred was a guy who really liked to keep to himself. He wasn't one to go causing trouble. He had texted me the night before to say there was something he wanted to tell me, and we were to talk the next day. That's why I went to the house in the first place.'

'And you have no idea what that was about?'

'No.'

'So it could have been anything, but maybe he had seen something suspicious or someone in the area.'

'Maybe. As I say, I don't know.'

'Do you know if he had a PC or laptop?'

'I'm not sure. It wouldn't surprise me if he didn't. He went to the library a lot.'

'We saw no computer in the house, but that might have been stolen. Recent search history is always a good source of information.'

Sullivan looked over at Mooney. 'Well, thanks for your time today, June. We'll be back in touch as the investigation proceeds. If you think of anything else, please do give us a call.' Sullivan handed me his card, and I saw the two of them out.

Sitting back down at the table, I let out a long, deep breath, aware that the time the detectives were with me I had been tensed up, my breathing shallow.

Sam came wandering downstairs and joined me at the table. A look of concern furrowed his usually untroubled brow.

'Cathy told me about Fred. That's so bad. What do they think happened?'

'They think he was attacked, but they're not sure why.'

Sam looked out the window as if that might provide some clues. 'But who would do that to someone as harmless as Fred?'

'That's the question that needs to be answered. Who would do something like that?' I was aware as I asked the question that I might even be probing to see if Sam had heard anything.

He looked up as if he had caught that nuance as well. I immediately felt guilty. Not that I had intended in any way to put him on the spot.

'Don't look at me. How would I know anything about that?'

I reached over and put my hand over his. 'Sorry, love. I

wasn't implying you would, more that you might have noticed something, or someone else might have said something. I don't know. I guess we're all pretty shaken.' Sam didn't reply, but he kept his hand where it was. I took comfort in that. If he was offended, he would have pulled it away. I was also relieved to have the reassurance of the contact with another human whom I loved. My head was spinning, and just the fact of that contact helped to ground me.

14

To say sleep was in short supply would be a gross understatement. It was almost non-existent. I felt scared and alone in bed. There was a killer out there, and nobody knew what they wanted or why they had done it. My alarm was set for eight, as I had fully intended going to work, but as it happened, I finally fell into a short, desperate sleep just after seven, so when the alarm went off, the most energy I could summon was to reach over, turn it off, and then just lie there, feeling like my limbs were weighed down with cement. I put a call into work and said I would do a bit from home. There was plenty of admin to do, so I could just chase up some of my cases. They were completely understanding, given the circumstances. One of my colleagues even offered to drop by and keep me company, but I declined. Kind as it was, I really didn't feel up to any social engagement.

As I lay there, I tried to imagine what would drive a person to commit such a terrible crime on someone like Fred. Admittedly, as someone who kept to himself so much, he had few friends, but at the same time, he had no enemies that I knew of. He was the typical, polite, mannerly neighbour who just wants to get on with their quiet life. When his wife, Margaret, was alive, they could be seen out and about a lot, but since she had died, Fred really lived the quiet life. So who would have done it? Was it a burglary that went wrong? Fred could have been a target, living completely alone and elderly. You heard of scammers who did the rounds, asking people if they wanted work done on their house and then forcing their way in to grab whatever valuables they could. Fred would have put up a fight if something like that happened. He wasn't one to back down.

That got me thinking of the row with Steve and how Fred had been so upset by Steve's boorish, inconsiderate behaviour. Maybe they had some interaction that I wasn't aware of, and it had spiralled out of control. Was that what he wanted to tell me?

I managed to roll out of bed after nine and make myself some breakfast. Cathy and Sam were up shortly after, but they did their typical breakfast on the hoof and rushed out the door with minutes to go before the first lecture. Cathy did pause before she left and ask if I was okay on my own, but I told her to go on.

That day passed in a blur, but towards evening, as I was doing some work on my laptop, I saw a car pull up outside Fred's house. A young man got out and looked at the house. It took me a minute to put the features together and recognize him as Fred's son, Cathal. He stayed outside and looked warily up the drive. I could almost read his thoughts. Actually going into the house was more than he could bear, so I went out to him.

'Hi, Cathal. You remember me, June Sweeney. I'm very sorry for what happened. It must be such an awful shock for you.'

Cathal was in his late twenties, dark haired, sallow

skinned, and had that sheen of invincibility the very young have, but I could see with this incident, it was fraying around the edges. His eyes had dark rings around them, and his movements were uncertain. This was new territory for all of us, but especially for a young man whose father had been murdered.

'Do you want me to go in with you?'

'Thanks. I'd appreciate that.' His voice had a brittleness to it. The two of us walked slowly up Fred's short driveway. Cathal had keys to the house, and he turned them slowly in the door. Before he opened it, he looked back at me.

'I heard it was you made the call to emergency services.'

'Yes, we were due to have a talk that evening. Fred was such a good neighbour.' I left out the bit about him texting me and saying we needed to talk. Cathal had enough troubles. He didn't need to know all that.

Cathal slowly pushed the front door open. He looked at some photos that were on a stand in the hallway; then he walked as far as the double doors and stopped. I rested a hand on his arm as he took in the view of the room where his dad had been killed. His gaze rested on the far wall, which Fred had covered with photos of himself, Margaret and Cathal. Cathal must have looked at them and seen a past that was out of his reach now.

As if to reinforce that idea, he turned to me. 'I don't feel any connection with the house anymore. It feels like somewhere I don't belong. I didn't know what I'd do when I was on my way over, but I know now. I have to sell the place. I can't bear the idea of what happened here.'

'I understand. You do whatever is right for you.'

We stood there another while. Cathal showed no inclination to go further into the house. I noticed that the mess that had been there on the day he was killed had been tidied. They had obviously collected all the evidence they could find and put the place back together as best they could.

I walked back out with Cathal.

'Thanks for coming in, June. I have an aunt who's going to get all the personal effects from the house. I'll be here till after the funeral.' His voice sounded detached, almost robotic. It must have been too much for him to process. He had to get out of there.

———

THE NEXT FEW days had an eerie quality to them. I saw the detectives come and go in the estate. Sometimes, they would sit in their car for what seemed like hours on end, and I wondered, were they observing the various comings and goings, or were they offering a kind of security? Either way, I was happy to see them. Whoever had done that to Fred was still out there. The quicker they got to the bottom of it and got the perpetrator, the better. As a single woman, I felt especially vulnerable.

Otherwise, life went on as normal in the estate. Steve was out with his cars, but he was keeping the music low for the moment. Philly and co. were still bringing their slabs of beer into the house, and Sam was over with them as much as ever.

I spotted Jim McCann one evening doing his rounds. He saw me out in the garden and came over, shaking his head.

'That was simply awful what happened to your neighbour. The whole street must be in shock.'

'Yes, it was really terrible to die in such a violent way, all alone.'

'Shocking.' McCann kept shaking his head. 'It's the kind of thing you hear about on the news, but you never expect it to come to your own back door.'

There was a lull in the conversation then. I felt like

McCann was doing his duty in offering his sympathy, so there wasn't much more to say about it.

'I heard the son was around. Very difficult for him. You can only imagine.'

'Yes, he's an only child. That makes it even harder.'

'He's going to sell up, apparently,' he continued. 'I think that's what any of us would do in the circumstances. Who could possibly live with those memories?'

'I suppose so.' I wasn't too happy at the idea of new neighbours coming in. There had been enough disturbance on the estate, but I understood that Cathal just wanted to make a clean break of it.

'There'll be plenty of interest in it. Might even get you thinking. Can't be easy living beside a house where something that terrible happened.'

'No.' That was true what he said, but the idea of moving because of it hadn't occurred to me.

I lay in bed that evening, thinking it all through. Was I going to be able to reconcile what had happened to Fred and stay living where I was? Maybe there was some sense in what McCann said. It wasn't going to be easy staying here. Would I always be thinking of what happened? If they caught whoever did it, that would be a good start. That brought me back to thinking about Fred's cryptic text the day before he was killed. Was there a connection? I wasn't sure I would ever know, but then what was he trying to say just before he died? It seemed to be one word, one with a strong *B* sound to it. It made no sense to me.

15

I was losing sight of what normality was, but I went back to work the next day, exhausted and emotionally drained. Sleep had become a luxury. Any time I did fall asleep, I would have short, intense nightmares where I was either trying to get back to my house or locked out of the house. I was desperate to get in and had this terrible sense, a foreboding sense, that something awful was about to happen. I would wake with a start and try to piece everything back together again. The trouble was, the reality of my situation was as bad as the nightmare. It was so difficult to comprehend what had happened and what was going on.

Dealing with other people's problems was something of a panacea. It took my mind off my own. However, when I arrived back home, Nick was in the kitchen, chatting with Sam. I just wanted to flake out after the day's work but had to run this newly imposed gauntlet.

'Well, any news on Fred?' was Nick's opening gambit.

Nick hadn't been around to console me after the murder or to see if I felt safe or needed any support, so I wasn't inclined to humour him.

'Nothing yet. They're going through routine procedure.'

'Oh. I wonder if they have a shortlist of suspects. That's normally the way they operate. Interview everyone and watch out for inconsistencies.' He looked pretty chuffed with his assessment. Sam was nodding in agreement.

'They stopped me on the way to college and asked who I was and then they asked me a few questions about what I saw that day. Have they spoken to you yet?'

'Me?' Nick looked surprised. 'No, I don't live here anymore. Why would they want to talk to me?'

I thought there was a little barb stuck in there with my name on it, but I chose to ignore it and went about making some gnocchi, which we'd have with the remains of a side of salmon I'd cooked the day before.

'But you work here these days,' Sam persisted.

'I suppose they'll come around to talking to me eventually. I suppose they have people who are much higher on the list to go through first.'

'It's scary to think there might be someone like that around, but they will have to talk to everyone. You never know what might trigger someone to act like that. It could be anyone, really,' I said.

Sam glowered at me. 'You're not trying to imply that Dad could be that someone, are you?'

'No, not in the least.' I was genuinely shocked that he would make that inference.

'Because sometimes, you seem like you don't think too much of Dad.'

'My God, Sam. I would never suspect your dad of doing something like that. How could you think that?'

'I don't know what to think, do I?'

Sam got up and left the room. Nick was looking at me. He stretched his hands apart in a gesture of disbelief. I wasn't quite buying the disbelief. Nick was very good at undermining my position in the household and seeking to further his own favour with the kids.

'It's a time of real stress for them,' he said. 'They're not going to admit it, but they'll have been seriously shook up by what happened to Fred.'

'As am I. I didn't notice you coming around to show much support.'

'I didn't want to get in the way. Besides, as I said to Sam, I don't live here anymore.'

'But you're happy to use the place for your own purposes and to drop in whenever it suits.'

I could see him stiffen. 'What I'm doing is for all of us,' he said with a clipped tone.

'To some extent, but it's mostly for you.' I regretted saying that as soon as it came out. A full-blown argument, raking over the coals of the past, was the last thing I wanted.

'Oh, really? So I'm the selfish one, as usual. You have it all nicely boxed off, don't you?' Nick jumped up, rinsed his mug, and took off out the door. I didn't say anything or try to stop him, happy enough that it had ended without a protracted row, but straight after he left, Sam came back into the kitchen.

'Dad left in a hurry, didn't he? Must have been something you said. As usual.' He grabbed a glass of water and left again.

I was feeling tired and besieged. The stress of the last few days was really starting to build. I sat in an armchair and looked out the window at the street. A couple of tears worked their way out of my eyes to slide down my cheeks. What had happened to our street? What was happening to the people around me? I felt alone and vulnerable. It felt like something sinister had come into our lives and was gutting us from the inside out.

I was glad to get to bed that night. It felt comforting to

close the bedroom door behind me, turn on my bedside light, and read a few pages of my book. Sam was in his room, supposedly studying but probably watching Netflix. I could hear tinny American accents coming through his bedroom door.

In a state of exhaustion, I fell into a deep sleep. No amount of fear or anxiety could keep me awake, I was so tired. Even as I was reading, my eyelids struggled to stay more than a sliver open.

I went for a very groggy pee at some stage. Everything in the house was dark and fuzzy. I turned on the little light over the wash-hand basin so I could see what I was doing. After I flushed, I noticed that the water in the toilet bowl swirled around for an age before slowly seeping out.

Oh, damn, I thought, *what's going on there? Maybe it's just low water pressure*. I really didn't want to entertain the idea of a blockage at that time of night, so I hoped for the best and went back to bed.

My fears of blockage were well founded, though. When I went to pee again first thing in the morning, the water level in the toilet seemed okay, but as soon as I flushed, the level kept rising and rising until it spilled over the side of the bowl and all over the floor.

'Curses,' I muttered to myself. 'This does look like a blockage.'

I stuck a note on the door, saying *do not use*, and checked the downstairs toilet. Same story. Somebody, probably Cathy, had used it in the night, and there was dirty water all over the floor. She had probably flushed and left straight away, so she wouldn't have seen what happened.

I called in to work, explained the situation and told them I'd be delayed, then phoned a plumber we'd used before. It took several calls to actually get through to him, and when I eventually did, he was, of course, up to his eyes. He only agreed to come when I started pleading with him, but he said it would be late afternoon.

I worked from home. There was a petrol station a few hundred yards up the road, and that was what we had to use while waiting for the plumber. The kids both had breakfast on the hoof and headed straight for college, so I was left alone again to ponder how one thing after another just seemed to be piling up. I scolded myself then, thinking of Fred and his poor son, Cathal, and how my troubles paled in comparison.

The plumber, Eddie, arrived at the absolute tail end of the afternoon. I had made several trips to the petrol station at that stage, feeling like some shadowy figure who was skulking in and out of the place. Eddie took a quick look at the upstairs and downstairs toilets and shook his head.

'Blockage.' He checked his watch. 'Not sure I'll have time to get to the root of it today.'

'My mother is coming to stay with me for a couple of days. I really need it sorted. She's elderly and infirm.' I was amazed how easily that lie slipped out, but there was no way I was letting him go without sorting it.

He checked his watch again and gave his head another shake, but he jogged out to his van and grabbed a box of tools, which I took to be a positive sign, so I just watched quietly. I heard him check the cisterns and then saw him go out the back where the pipes flow. There was the sound of drain covers being lifted and then what sounded like dragging and heaving.

'June,' he called from the back.

I went out to him and saw he was holding a filthy, soggy bag of cement in his hands. He looked at me as if I might be able to explain the bag of cement, but I must have looked suitably confused.

'Somebody put this down your outflow pipe. Luckily, it

hadn't burst open. If it had, you'd be looking at a serious problem.'

'But why would anyone do that?'

Eddie shrugged. 'Beats me. Did you cross somebody recently?'

'Not that I know of.' I started thinking of the bin and the car alarm and wondered, could it be the same person?

Eddie charged me just for the call-out. He looked glad to be on his way, no big delays. He took the cement bag with him, saying he would dump it. He reckoned whoever put it there might try to use it again if it was left. When he said that, I felt a chill deep in my stomach. There was obviously someone out there who was targeting me, and they were still out there, close enough to make a move whenever they wanted. Was it just the one person doing it all the time, or was there more than one involved? And the biggest question, the one I was really struggling to find an answer to, was why? Was it connected in any way to Fred's death, or was that just coincidence? If it was connected to Fred, then what did they want? Who would go to such extremes, and what were they looking for? If it wasn't connected with Fred, then what was it connected with?

I started brooding over who would do this to me and drawing up my own list of suspects. Steve was, of course, number one. He had all the motivation, unhappy with the way we had treated him since he arrived, the way Paul had gone for him, and I had complained to McCann. He didn't seem like a remorseful character at all, so he wouldn't see that it was his own behaviour that was causing the friction. He would just see us as troublesome, meddling neighbours who were interfering with his life.

Then there was Nick. He was never to be underestimated in how far he'd go to get his own way. Did he want me out of the house so he could get his money and buy somewhere with his partner? The answer to that was a resounding yes, but would he stoop to behaviour as low as that? I didn't have a clear answer for that. I had been surprised many times by how low he would stoop. Maybe this was him pushing into new territory.

I even briefly thought of Sam. It seemed very doubtful he would do a thing like that, but the way he had been acting towards me, with increasing resentment, especially with my attitude towards Nick, I had to give the idea some consideration. He was a good kid, but smoking a lot of weed might have really distorted his thinking.

Then again, if it was connected to Fred's murder, all of the above were off the table, except maybe Steve. He did have a criminal past and had shown himself to be well capable of violence, but why would he go so far as to kill someone as harmless as Fred?

16

There had been no news on the investigation into Fred's death, but the Gardai had been back around to me, looking for Nick's contact number. They knew he was doing work in the area and wanted to 'eliminate him from their enquiries'. I passed his number on, glad to see that they were being thorough in their investigation. With the incidents that had happened to me, I was, of course, upset, but nothing compared with the death of Fred. Disturbed as I was by the incidents, I was even more frightened at the idea they might be linked to Fred's death.

I knew the Gardai would give nothing away until they had something concrete, so I wasn't at all surprised when they told me they were continuing with their enquiries and how every piece of information they received was vital to the investigation.

I decided to talk to Sam about the blockage, as it was on my mind that he had some sort of growing grudge against me that seemed to be connected with Nick. I wasn't sure, but I wanted to tease it out.

I waited until after dinner when he seemed relaxed. He

said he was going over to Philly's later that night, so I picked a time when he was down in the kitchen, making himself some hot chocolate.

'You know the toilet blockage that we had,' I said.

'Yeah?' His reply was more of a question than an affirmative.

'Well, they discovered it wasn't a fault in the system. It was a malicious act.'

'Malicious?' He had just grabbed his hot chocolate from the microwave.

'Yes, somebody put a bag of cement in the outflow pipe.'

That made him frown. 'A what in the what?'

'A bag of cement was used to block the flow of sewage. Somebody wanted to stink our house out of it.'

The frown stayed put. 'Who would do a thing like that?'

'I haven't a clue, and that's what bothers me. I would suspect, though, that it is the same person who set the bin on fire and also set off my car alarm.'

I could see him hesitate with the hot chocolate. He had probably intended to bring it upstairs and watch Netflix, but he slid his mug onto the table and sat down.

'Why are you bringing it up with me?'

'Well, you're young. You've got a different perspective on things, so I wanted to hear your ideas.'

He shook his head and made his fringe of curls swish from side to side. He finished the gesture with a shrug. 'I don't know. How would I know anything about it?'

'As I said, you might have some different ideas. Two heads are better than one.'

The frown returned. 'I hope you don't think it was anything to do with me.'

'Of course not.'

'You've been making some accusations lately, particularly

at Dad. He even told me you gave the police his number so they could contact him.'

I felt the beginnings of an argument rumble on the horizon. *Well, thanks, Nick,* I thought to myself, *for adding even more fuel to the fire.*

'They asked me for his number. I was hardly going to say no.'

Sam digested this piece of information, taking a swig from his hot chocolate and wiping his mouth with the back of his hand afterwards.

'Still, you're not making things easy for Dad, are you? He said he has to move out of his place, and they need money for somewhere new, so why can't we sell up if it helps him?'

'Oh, so he told you all that? It should really be something between me and him. It's not fair to involve you guys in stuff like that.'

Sam grabbed his mug and stood up. 'Why not? It's something we should all have a say in. I don't see why we have to stay here. We could easily have a smaller house. Cathy will be gone soon, and so will I, so why not? But maybe you don't want to help Dad out because of some old grudge or whatever.'

I was certainly not going to get into my history with Nick, so I let it slide and watched Sam disappear upstairs. My chat with him hadn't yielded anything apart from the fact that Nick now seemed to be telling him everything. What exactly was Nick up to? He had never got Sam so heavily involved before. In fact, for a time after we split, he had hardly seen the kids at all because he was so wrapped up in his new life. Still, it started me thinking. Maybe I was just being stubborn hanging onto the house. Perhaps it was time to at least give selling up some consideration. There was nothing to lose in thinking about it.

Later that evening, I spotted Jim McCann coming out of

his nephew, Philly's house. I took the opportunity to pop out and have a quick chat.

'Any developments in the case with Fred?' he asked as soon as he saw me.

'Not that I know of. They're taking statements from everyone, so I guess they'll see what they have at the end of that.'

'Sure. Let's hope they make some quick progress. Can't be easy for you, knowing there's someone like that around.'

'No. Not at all, and there's been a few strange happenings.'

'The bin?'

'Yeah, that and a bit more. It kind of leads me to a question I wanted to ask, like if I was thinking of selling up, what sort of money do you think I'd get?'

McCann looked around the estate and shook his head. 'I mean, in normal times, you would be looking at a good price, but with what's been going on and poor Fred, I don't know if it would get quite what you deserve. It's a fine estate and good, solid houses. I could have a chat with a couple of people and get back to you.'

'Sure, yeah, that'd be good.' It wasn't quite what I wanted to hear, but there was no denying recent events would have an effect on the price. When I looked over at Steve's and saw the oil stains everywhere and the cars up on blocks, waiting to be worked on, I could see it through the eyes of a buyer, and it wasn't a pretty sight, and then there was Fred. That was certainly going to tarnish anyone's view of the place, even if it was just a random break-in that had gone wrong.

McCann paused before getting into his car. 'I know it can't be easy for you, June. This must all be very frightening and disturbing. I can see you're a strong woman, but I'd like to say that I'm there for you if you ever need anything. We don't know each other that well, but I have a lot of respect for someone who manages all that you do. It can't be easy.'

I was a little taken aback by that, and I'm pretty sure I blushed. 'Thanks for that. Yeah, it's not easy. We just muddle on as best we can, don't we?'

McCann laughed. 'You do the muddling bit pretty well from where I'm standing. Maybe you could give classes in muddling. We could all do with a bit of advice on that front.'

I laughed too and headed back into the house. It was nice to get some positive attention for a change, even if it was from someone I hardly knew.

Cathy was in briefly for some food, then announced she was heading over to babysit at Steve's. She hadn't been for a good few days, so I resisted the urge to tell her not to be late back.

Unfortunately, she was late, very late. In fact, I'm pretty sure dawn was making its presence felt by the time she got back. She had college next day at ten, so I had to call her multiple times from work to get her up. She answered eventually at a quarter past ten. I didn't give out to her because her voice sounded so tired and croaky, but I wasn't happy. The little hiatus when she hadn't been going over was a relief. I had even hoped that the whole thing would fizzle out, but no such luck.

I mentioned the lateness to her next evening. She was on her way out to meet friends.

'It depends what time he gets back, doesn't it?' she had answered.

'You have to think of college and the life you are hoping to make for yourself.'

'There are other considerations too, Mam.' She left that sentence hanging in the air. I wasn't sure what to say. Did I want to know what she meant by 'other considerations'?

She hurried out the door. I was glad that at least she was going out with her college friends. After she had left, I heard music coming from Steve's. Looking out the window, I could see he was working on one of his cars, door open again. He was stopping to vape every now and then as he worked, big clouds of smoke billowing up. I noticed that he had his front gate closed, and then I saw why. The two dogs were charging around his front garden. Every now and then, one of them would put its front paws up on the wall and survey the street, mouth open to reveal rows of fierce teeth. It looked very like the low wall wouldn't contain them if they saw something they didn't like. I was definitely not going out to do my garden with those two chasing around.

Steve had been quiet since Fred's death, probably aware that the Gardai would be making regular rounds of the estate. Now he seemed to be back in full swing, worse than ever. I wondered if it was even legal to have dogs like that running around a front garden. It was something I'd have to bring up with McCann. No way was I going to be a prisoner in my own house.

17

N ext day when I got back from work, I saw that Steve had added another car to his collection. That meant two in his drive and two outside. The two in his drive took up so much room that he couldn't close the gates over. The second car was sticking out, so it took up half the footpath. I sincerely hoped he wouldn't be letting the dogs out, as they would not be penned in.

I didn't see them but couldn't hear their usual barking and snuffling on the other side of the gate, as Steve had the music up loud. It was a messy and chaotic scene, but I didn't want to risk a confrontation with Steve, so I took the step of calling McCann again.

'June,' he said as soon as he answered.

'It's about Steve. He's made even more of a mess outside. He had the dogs out in the front yesterday, and I'm afraid he'll let them out again. But even if he doesn't, it's a horrific mess.'

'I understand, June.' With his soft voice, it sounded like he really did understand. 'I'll be over later. I was going to call in to you anyway to follow up on our chat the other night.'

I passed the time while I was waiting for McCann as best I could, trying not to get too worked up by Steve. Sam wandered in, oblivious apparently to the racket and the mess outside. He was being quiet and truculent after our interaction the other night. It left me wondering what Nick might have been saying to him, but I really wasn't in the mood for any more negativity, so I directed Sam to a beef casserole that I had defrosted. He helped himself to it, ear pods in to minimize the threat of conversation. I let him at it, sat in an armchair, and struggled to concentrate on an in-depth article on the state of social services that I had spotted in the review section of the paper. I had a habit of buying the paper on a Saturday but only getting round to reading the articles bit by bit over the week.

Once Sam went out, my powers of concentration improved. I had just Tammy for company, purring restlessly on the couch. She was doing that scratchy thing again, digging her claws into the upholstery and pulling at it. I tried to block that out, having resigned myself years ago to having little tears in the upholstery. There wasn't a whole lot I could do, so I had chosen thick, black, velvety material so at least she wouldn't damage the sofa underneath.

McCann rapped on the door about eight. He was looking fresh and cheery with a boyish energy that never seemed to fade.

'All good?' he asked chirpily.

'Not really.' I nodded towards Steve's place and the multiplying cars.

McCann rubbed his chin as if he were thrown into deep thought. 'I know. I've spoken to him on a few occasions, and he assures me every time that he's on the cusp of getting premises.'

'I know there's only so much you can do. Hopefully, he does get those premises soon.' I realized Steve would be a tough nut to crack. I stood aside to make space and gestured inside. 'Listen, why don't you come in? I was just about to crack open a nice bottle of red.' I wasn't sure where that last bit came from, but I suddenly had a desire for a good glass of wine in the company of another adult.

'Very kind of you, if you're sure I'm not imposing.'

He followed me in, and I picked one of my Languedocs, a sure bet for most tastes. McCann sipped appreciatively at the generous glass I poured. 'Mmm, nice. I'm driving, though, so better watch the quantities.'

He had sat on the couch near Tammy. I went back to my armchair. The wine slid easily down my throat, and I felt the troubles of the world begin to slide off my shoulders.

'As I was saying last night, you manage your situation here admirably. I'm not sure I'd have as steady a hand as you.'

'You get used to it. Practice makes perfect, or imperfect might be more accurate.'

He laughed. 'You're not wrong. Perfection is the rock so many have perished on.' He took a long, appreciative sip from his wine. His boyish features scrunched up as he did. I felt I could see him on a cricket pitch or sailing a yacht, something well-heeled and outdoorsy. His skin had a soft all-year tan to it like someone who spent a lot of time in the sun but looked after themselves at the same time.

'Now, you were asking about selling the house and what the current climate is like,' he continued. 'I've been thinking it through, and I spoke to the landlord who is purchasing properties in the area.' Here he sucked his cheeks in like something sour had suddenly attacked his taste buds. 'Unfortunately, with what happened next door and with the antisocial behaviour on the street, he feels the price may not be that good. However, if you decided you were interested in selling, I can certainly put a good word in and bump it up as much as possible.'

I felt immediately deflated by that summary of the situation, but I was determined not to show it. Drinking wine in the company of someone who was easy on the eye was a novelty for me. I thought I'd worry about the house stuff another time. Tammy was beside McCann on the couch, and he gave her the odd rub, to which she purred in response. She started doing her claw thing, though, getting dangerously near to his legs, so I pulled her off and placed her on the floor. She looked back at the place she had commanded and looked like she might jump back up again.

'Why don't you sit here,' he said, patting the place beside him. 'That way she won't be able to claw the sofa.'

I smiled and felt like a debutante on her first date, but I grabbed my glass of wine and sat down. He smiled at me and rested a hand in the space between us. I was aware of him, his looks, his warmth and the fact that he was working his charm on me. I was aware but didn't mind. It had been so long since anyone had bothered to do exactly that. I was willing to run with it and see where it brought us.

'So, tell me, June, how is it that someone young and attractive like you is still single?' He laughed after saying that, knowing that we were both aware he was playing the charm card to its fullest extent.

I laughed too, appreciating the frankness and the humour at the same time. 'Well, it wouldn't by any chance be anything to do with the fact that I have buckets of responsibility and two overgrown children running around the place, would it?'

'Your kids are nice. I see quite a lot of Sam over at Philly's place. He's just a typical laddish teen who'll come out of his shell in his own good time.'

'It's been quite a time, but yeah, I know he's sweet under all the anger.'

'So if that's not your excuse for being single, then what is? You just not bothered?'

'I don't know. Maybe. After all the hassle with Nick, I'd be very cautious.'

'Too cautious, perhaps?' He shunted over a little on the sofa so we were sitting closer. I could feel his body warmth and was aware of his strong, tanned hands just inches away from me.

I laughed again. 'Hopefully not. Anyway, that's enough about me. What's your story?' I hadn't heard him mention a wife or partner.

He smiled and shook his head. 'I'm one of those types who has to keep moving. I was abroad for a while, hence the tan.' He held his tanned arm up close to my face for inspection. His skin was a soft brown colour, the muscles on his arm well-defined. 'I've always been in the property game, and it's taken me all over.'

'A girl in every port, then?'

'Not quite. There's been some flings here and there, but nothing long term.'

I guessed he had probably been selling apartments somewhere hot like Spain or Portugal but felt I'd asked enough.

'People see me with the tan and the Merc, and they might figure I have this free and easy lifestyle, but it's not all it's cracked up to be.'

'Should I get out the violins, then?'

He laughed and put his hand on mine. I felt a jolt of static electricity run through me, and it took all my power not to pull my hand away, not because I objected but because I was so unused to someone actually touching me like that. He smiled at me and leaned in closer. I could feel the warmth of his face close to mine. Then he moved a little closer still, and our lips met in the middle. He brushed his lips gently off mine, and I felt a tingle rise from my stomach.

'That was nice,' he said, pulling slowly way.

'It was,' I managed to say, although I might have half-croaked the words. Then we leaned back into each other and let our lips brush slowly against each other. His breath was sweet with a hint of mint flavour. I had seen him smoking before, so I guessed the mints were part of the whole package. He put his hand behind my back and began to run it up and down my spine, gently, but not too gently, so I could feel his fingers running smoothly into all the little dips and crevices. The tingling in my stomach was starting to build. I could feel small waves running in flushing pulses, gaining strength all the time. He moved closer again, but just as he did, I heard a key turn in the door, and Sam came strolling in, oblivious to the world, the tinny sound of loud music leaking from his ear pods. He stopped briefly in the hall to take his jacket off. In that moment, we sprang apart so we were sitting at opposite ends of the sofa like two teenagers who had been caught by a parent.

I think I brushed myself quickly down as Sam walked in. He stopped in his tracks, stared at the two of us, and smiled enigmatically, but he left the ear pods in as he got himself a glass of water and retreated upstairs.

We looked sheepishly at each other and laughed quietly.

'I guess that puts a halt to things,' McCann said.

'Unfortunately, yes.'

'I'll call again.'

'Please do.'

We walked awkwardly together towards the hall door, which I opened to let him out. He looked around the houses as he left.

'I hope things settle down for you here.'

'Me too. I really hope they get whoever killed Fred.'

He shook his head wistfully. 'Poor guy. Nobody deserves to die like that. He must have been such a good husband when his wife was alive.'

'He was completely devoted. It was so sad when she died.'

'All the photos of his wife, like every moment of their life was displayed.'

I remembered all the photos he had around the mantelpiece and the far wall and nodded in agreement. 'They were devoted to each other. In a way, it's good Margaret didn't live to see what happened, sad as it is to say that.'

'I know exactly what you mean.'

We paused at the door, I guess each of us wondering how to finish.

'Listen, thanks for a nice evening. Hopefully, we'll get to do it again.' He winked at me and walked briskly to his car. I watched him take off in his Merc, his face and tousled hair as boyish as ever.

Going back inside, I sipped at the remains of my wine. The little encounter had been very pleasant, but as I thought about McCann's parting remarks, a sense of disquiet began to envelop me. He had said how sad it was about Fred's death and then commented on how devoted a husband he had been, based on the photos on Fred's wall and mantelpiece. The trouble with that was, to the best of my knowledge, he had never been inside Fred's house. The photos were down the far end of the kitchen-cum-living room, therefore far away from the window at the front. They could only be seen from inside the house. Fred had expressed his distrust of McCann, and I knew Fred as a man of his word. If he didn't trust someone, he would have no dealings with them, certainly not let them into his house. The feeling of disquiet grew.

I searched for an explanation. Perhaps someone had told McCann about the photos, but who was it if they did? Fred was such a private man, so few people would have been inside his house. Maybe that couple who had come looking to buy houses had been let in, but that seemed a bit unlikely. Fred had said he hadn't entertained the idea of selling to them. Even if they had got in, they hadn't any connection to McCann that I was aware of.

Maybe McCann had done his research on Fred and found out as much as he could about his background. Perhaps that was part of his modus operandi as an agent for whoever this landlord was who wanted to buy up property on our street. If that was the case, maybe that was why he was interested in coming into my house, and the rest was all just a façade. But worse, much worse . . . was it in some way connected to the killing of Fred? That lingering thought left me with a very sleepless night.

18

Thinking about what McCann had said troubled me into the next day. There was something not right about it, whatever angle I looked at it from. How or why did he know about the photos in Fred's front room?

That led me back to thinking about the day Fred died. He had been trying to say something to me. I had only made out some sort of *B* sound, no more. What was he trying to tell me? At the time, I thought maybe he could have been saying a name, but it could have been the name of a family member. Fred was seriously injured, so his thought processes would have been severely impaired. But that moment kept coming back to me. What if he was trying to tell me something about who killed him or why?

I got a text from McCann later in the day, saying, 'Thanks for last night, really enjoyed it. Pity about the interruption.' I didn't reply. The unsettling feeling was too strong. He wasn't getting into my house again.

That evening, I had both Sam and Cathy for dinner. It was coming to the end of term, and they had lots of work to finish up. I felt comforted that they were both there for the night, but towards the end of dinner, Cathy got a ping on her phone and checked it.

'It's Steve. He needs me to babysit. Something urgent has come up for him.'

'But you have your work to do. I'm sure he can find someone else.'

'No, Mam, not at such short notice. Besides, I can get the work done over there. The girls will be in bed early. They've got school in the morning.'

I didn't like the idea of Cathy going over to Steve's. The night before and the day had been too unsettling. I didn't know what was going on. On top of that, I was afraid Sam might decide to go out, and then I would be alone. That prospect made me distinctly nervous. I still had so much to figure out before I felt safe. However, I knew there was no point taking it up with Cathy. It would probably just end in an argument and her doing it anyway.

'Okay, love. Just don't be late.'

Cathy headed out about a half hour later. Sam retreated to his room without saying anything about going out. That was some relief, anyway.

I spent the evening watching Netflix, catching up on one of the Scandinavian dramas. I was absorbed by the fine acting and the storyline, but at the same time, I wondered if a murder mystery was the type of thing I should be watching.

Sam's light was off by eleven when I went upstairs to start getting ready for bed. *He must be wrecked*, I thought, *between all the socializing and the pressure of college work.*

I had a shower, then spent a bit of time rubbing in moisturizer, brushing my hair, generally trying to make myself as fresh and presentable as I could for the next day. I find a bit of extra effort the night before can lead to surprising dividends the day after. I took my book to bed then, allowing myself to drift into a cosy, sleepy mode. Cathy wasn't in yet. I hoped to hear the front door open and close shortly. She needed a good night's sleep.

I was just about to turn off my lamp and drift off to sleep when I heard the cat flap open and close in the front door.

That's odd, I thought. Tammy had been in and sleeping beside me as I watched Netflix. She looked so cosy when I left, it would have surprised me if she'd gone out so soon. *That's cats for you,* I thought and dismissed it, turning the lamp off and settling in to sleep.

Before I could properly close my eyes, I heard what sounded like Tammy hissing. *That's very strange,* I thought. *Maybe a rodent or something came in the cat flap.* Wearily, I pulled myself out of bed and started to make my way downstairs. I grabbed a small pencil torch I keep beside my bed because I didn't want to start turning lights on in case it woke Sam.

Making my way down the stairs, I could hear Tammy hissing in the hallway. Shining my torch on her, I could see her back was arched, and she was hissing in the direction of our downstairs toilet. Turning my torchlight in that direction, I was just in time to see some sort of tail disappear around the door.

'Oh, my God, what's that?' I heard myself saying. I froze where I was on the stairs, unable to move. Was that some sort of large rat? Whatever it was, the tail was long. I didn't know what to do. All I knew was I wasn't going anywhere near that downstairs toilet on my own. Reluctantly, I crept back upstairs and knocked on Sam's door. I really didn't want to wake him, but this was an emergency.

He appeared after a few muffled protests, rubbing his eyes as he opened the door.

'What is it, Mam? I was asleep.'

'Something has just come in the cat flap. It's in the downstairs toilet.'

Sam looked at me, trying to make sense of what I was saying. 'It's what?'

'In the downstairs toilet. There's something. I saw a tail.'

Sam shook his head, probably trying to wake up and see if this was really happening. 'I'll go and have a look.' His voice was croaky with tiredness, but he took my pencil torch and headed down. Tammy was still in the hall. She was hissing quietly but showed no sign of going into the toilet after whatever was in there.

Sam approached the door slowly. He reached inside to turn the light on. I went down a few steps to get closer, but I wasn't going into the hall in case whatever it was came flying out. I could see Sam shining the torch towards the back of the toilet.

'Oh, crap,' he said and lurched back. 'There's something coiled up at the back of the toilet. It looks like a snake.'

'A snake?' I had to rummage in my mind for the image of a snake that might be hiding out in our toilet. Nothing came. It didn't compute. What would a snake be doing there? Tentatively, I walked towards the door. Sam stood back and handed me the flashlight. He gestured towards the back of the toilet. Meanwhile, Tammy approached as well, continuing with her low hissing sound.

I stuck my head slowly around the toilet door and scanned the area to the right of the toilet bowl, where I saw nothing. I put my head in that bit further, my heart thumping in my chest. There at the very back, between the toilet and the wall, I could see concentric rows of something curled up. It was grey and brown in colour with patches of yellow towards the top. The torch nearly fell out of my hand, but I retreated slowly and closed the door. Tammy stopped hissing but sat where she was in the hall, staring at the door.

'Oh, my God, how did that get in here?' I said, looking at Sam.

He shrugged. 'Some people keep pet snakes. It must have escaped.'

'But to come in through our cat flap?'

'I think they look for somewhere warm.'

I almost laughed at that. Sam was approaching the issue from a very practical angle. He looked like he just wanted to get back to bed.

'But it's a snake. In our house. What are we going to do?'

He shrugged again. 'Call the DSPCA in the morning, I suppose.'

I supposed he was right, but it didn't exactly calm me down. I didn't relish the prospect of sharing the house with a snake for the night. Also, I was very concerned about how it got in. Did somebody put it there? It seemed unlikely to me that suddenly, out of the blue, a snake would come sliding through our cat flap. I felt it was probably related to everything that was going on. To me, it seemed more likely to be a malicious act.

'It's safe for the moment, Mam.' Sam gestured towards the closed toilet door. I looked at the bottom and the top of the door and saw only a sliver of space. The snake I had seen was much more than a sliver. Sam was right. No way was the snake coming out of there.

'Okay, you go to bed. I'll call you if I need you.'

Sam seemed more than happy to head back to bed. I went into the kitchen and made myself a calming cup of chamomile tea. Tammy followed me in and jumped up on the sofa. She stared over at me like she was waiting for an explanation.

I sipped at the tea and felt its warmth settle me. The snake was safe where it was. Then a thought occurred to me. I had seen Cathy's bedroom door was open. She wasn't home. What would happen if she came home and opened the toilet door, as she might well do, not wanting to make noise upstairs? I thought about texting her, but she was sometimes very slow to get back. This situation required a deal more urgency. I wanted to be able to go back to bed and get some sleep. I realized I was going to have to call over to Steve's and tell her in person. That prospect unsettled me again. It was about the last thing I wanted to do, but I knew I had no choice.

Steeling myself, I checked the toilet door again and saw it was firmly closed. No sound issued from the other side. I got my house keys and slipped out the front door. The estate was deathly quiet. There was just the gentlest of winds that brushed off the plants and the hedges. Streetlights cast a yellow tinge on everything. As I walked towards Steve's, I could see the hulks of his various cars strewn at angles in and around his drive. I listened for the snuffling of the dogs on the other side of his gate but heard nothing.

There were lights on in the front room of his house, and I could hear low music as I approached. Taking a deep breath, I pressed his doorbell and heard a faint, musical sound in response. From somewhere inside, I heard a dog barking. My stomach fluttered with nerves as I waited. Finally, I heard footsteps approach the door, and it swung open to reveal Steve in a T-shirt, jeans, and bare feet. His hair looked ruffled.

'June?'

'I'm looking for Cathy. I need to tell her something.'

Steve pursed his lips as if he had to think about that. 'Do you want me to pass a message on to her?'

'No, I'd prefer to tell her myself.'

'Oh, is it something urgent?' Steve had a smile that was slowly creeping across his face. He wasn't making this easy for me, and he seemed to be enjoying it.

'Yes, it is. Cathy is my daughter, and I'd like to talk to her. Now.'

Behind Steve, I could see down the hall to a door that was

closed. From the other side of the door, I could hear the snuffling of his brutish dogs.

'Are you sure you don't want me to pass a message on to her? Might be easier.'

'We have a snake in our house. I need to tell Cathy. I want to tell her in person. Now, can you get her out, please?'

'A snake?' The smile widened. 'I wonder how that got in.'

'How it got in doesn't matter. It's there. Now, will you call Cathy?'

'She's upstairs,' he said succinctly, and I felt my heart drop like a stone.

'Upstairs?' I echoed.

'Yeah. In the sack, if you know what I mean. We were kind of in the middle of things.'

'I need to speak to my daughter,' I said forcefully, but Steve just chuckled.

'Your daughter is a grown woman who happens to be in a relationship with a grown man who happens to be me. If she comes down or not is her choice, but I am telling you she may not be too happy about it. Cathy likes her time upstairs, if you know what I mean. She's very enthusiastic, June. You know what? I think she might even be ready to have kids. How do you fancy being a granny?'

'She'll get tired of you. You're nothing but a troublemaker.'

'Now, that's not very nice, June. I may seem tough on the outside, but I have feelings.'

'You have no regard for other people's feelings, though, do you?'

'Well, that's not what Cathy thinks. She finds me very sensitive. In every way, if you get me.'

He was leering at me. I felt so frustrated and at the same time so worried for Cathy.

'You just remember that she is my daughter, and I will do everything I can to protect her.'

'Strong words, June, but I think I'll be doing a lot of the looking after now. In terms of tonight, I think you can rest easy with the snake. Cathy is well settled in upstairs. She won't be back tonight.' Steve leered at me again and winked before closing the door.

I think I stood in his doorway for a few seconds, trying to process what I had just experienced. I felt weak, and when I did move, I found that my legs were shaky and unsteady.

Walking back to my own house, my whole world suddenly felt very different. It felt like it had slipped away from my grasp. I no longer knew what I was dealing with. Steve had had more than lust in his eye when he told me Cathy was upstairs with him. There was something nasty and vindictive there too. He had a firm hold over me now, and he was letting me know. My daughter had effectively been taken hostage, but she had gone of her own free will.

19

I listened out for Cathy or for any sound of movement from the toilet for a long time before I fell into a deep, short sleep. In my dreams, I felt like something was pressing down on me, stopping me from breathing. I woke early, gasping for air, sitting bolt upright in bed, trying to make sense of where I was. It took a few long seconds to piece it all back together again.

'Cathy. The snake,' I said aloud and scrambled from the bed. Cathy's door was still open. She hadn't come home. My legs felt weak again, but I had to take a deep breath and make my way downstairs. The toilet door was firmly closed, and Tammy was sleeping on a mat in the hall. I guessed she had put herself there in case the snake decided to move.

I called the DSPCA as soon as the clock hit nine a.m.

'You have a what in your toilet?'

'A snake.'

'Do you know what type?'

I described it as best I could, and they seemed to relax after that. 'We'll be out as soon as we can. Just leave it where it is, and you'll be fine.'

I had to put a call in to work to tell them I would be late. Again. I was starting to feel very guilty for all the time I was taking off, not to mention neglectful of my clients. These were kids in desperate need of intervention, yet I was stuck at home, trying to sort my own life out.

The DSPCA arrived around ten thirty in overalls with a net and a long pole. I showed them to the toilet. There was a bit of scuffling and movement from inside, but they emerged a couple of minutes later with the snake wriggling in a bag.

'There we go,' one of them said cheerily, 'a grass snake, completely harmless, but that was quite a big one.'

'It came in through the cat flap,' I said. 'Would that be a normal thing to happen?'

'Normal? No, but we're used to dealing with the abnormal. You'd be amazed what people do with their pets. This one obviously got loose and went looking for somewhere to hide out.'

'It's just there's been a few things happening around, and I'm trying to make sense of it.'

The guy looked at me and tilted his head to one side as if to indicate he'd listen to whatever else I had to say, but I figured I had said enough. He'd done his bit, and it wasn't for me to burden him with anything else.

'No, it's nothing. You know yourself that when something like that happens, you wonder.'

'It could be someone playing a prank, and to be honest, it wouldn't be the first time we've had a call-out for a snake like that. But you did the right thing by calling us. We'll try to find it a new home.'

They headed off with the wriggling bag, and I was left at the table to mull through what had happened. The snake had slipped rapidly back down the hierarchy of worries I had. Maybe somebody had put it through the cat flap, and maybe it was related to the campaign of apparent intimidation against me, but worry on a whole new level was being generated by that scene with Steve the night before. The implications of what he had said were horrendous and designed to be hurtful to me. He was glorying in the fact that he had seduced Cathy and implying that he had her twisted around his little finger. Was this part of an intimidation tactic? Had he literally taken my daughter hostage?

I had the opportunity to sound this out at twelve o'clock when Cathy finally returned. She breezed into the house like nothing was wrong, gathering her stuff for college.

'You had a snake in the house?' she asked with a wrinkled nose as she grabbed a quick coffee and piece of toast.

'Yes, a grass snake, don't know how it got in.'

'Oh. That's weird.'

'Very. I had to call over to let you know not to go into the downstairs toilet.'

'Oh, yeah. Thanks. You could've just left a note on the door, though.'

'It wasn't exactly a situation I am used to. I didn't know what to do, but I wanted to make sure the snake didn't get out.' My tone was clipped. I could feel a knot of tension in my stomach and a wave of anger rising.

'No,' Cathy said ambivalently and took a swig of coffee.

'When I called to Steve's, you were upstairs, and he didn't seem keen to let me talk to you.'

'Well, it was late.'

'It's not the late bit that bothered me. It was the way he spoke about you, like he controlled you or something.'

Cathy laughed and sprayed a bit of coffee in the process. 'Controlled me? Come on, Mam, this isn't like the 1950s. I am an independent woman.'

'He is much older than you and has a lot of experience of life. I didn't like his attitude towards you.'

'Well, Mam, that's something between me and him, isn't it? I don't go getting involved with you and Dad, do I?'

Oh, God, I thought, *not the old Nick question again.* It seemed like the kids were using my broken relationship with Nick against me.

'There was no big age difference between me and Nick. What happened just happened. I don't want to go into it.'

'Well, there you go. You just said there was no big age difference between you two, and look what happened, so age has nothing to do with it.'

I felt like thumping the table in frustration. I could see that Cathy would do anything she could to justify her behaviour.

'I am just concerned for you, as someone who is starting out in life and has so much to look forward to. Steve even said you might think about having children together.'

'Did he?' She looked nonplussed and shrugged.

'Yes, he did, and I sincerely hope you are not thinking about that because that would be all your college years down the drain.'

Cathy studied her coffee as if it had suddenly become a focus of great interest. 'Life versus college, I suppose,' she said, still looking into the mug.

'You've always been strong-minded and know what you want, and a satisfying career has always been very much on your radar, so I would think long and hard about any changes you're thinking of making to that plan.'

Cathy stopped studying the inside of her mug and brought it to the sink to rinse it out. 'I always think long and hard, Mum, but maybe I don't always come up with the results that other people want.'

'Cathy, I am worried about you and your involvement with an older man who has a criminal background. It's as simple as that. I am not one to make judgement easily or to lecture other people on how they should live their lives, but you are very young still, and choices you make at this stage can affect you for the rest of your life.'

'Oh, so it's the background thing again, is it? If you don't judge, then why are you judging him?'

With that she went upstairs, got her bag ready for college, and left.

I sat where I was at the table and watched her leave. There was a sense that she had moved into new territory, and I wasn't sure what to do. I felt very alone. Cathy had turned against me or, at least, against what I wanted her to do. Sam seemed to have moved away from me and was blaming me for the separation with Nick. He seemed to think I was treating Nick badly.

Thinking about it, I decided that Nick should get involved. Cathy, after all, was his daughter, and he had to face his responsibilities, so I sent him a text saying we needed to talk.

He pulled up a couple of hours later. I had done some work online but had to get into the office in the afternoon, so time was precious.

'Well?' he said as an opener once he was sitting down.

'It's Cathy. This thing with Steve seems to be very serious. I had an incident last night where a grass snake slid through the cat flap, and I had to go over to warn Cathy. She was in bed with Steve. He said some things that weren't very complimentary about her and mentioned they might even be thinking of having kids together.'

'What?' Nick looked genuinely surprised. 'Having kids together? She's much too young for that.'

'And his background. He's got a criminal past, as we discussed before.'

Nick put his hands palm down on the table. 'I know about the past, and I think we said everyone needs a second chance.

I know him now from being around. He's actually done a bit of work on my pickup. He's rough around the edges, but he's not a bad guy. It's more the age thing that would bother me. Cathy is just starting out in life.'

'It's both things that would bother me. Everyone deserves a second chance, but the way he has behaved since coming to the estate doesn't indicate that he has changed much, in my opinion.'

Nick nodded as if in agreement. 'I can see where you're coming from, but at the same time, what are we going to do?'

'Talk to her, anyway. Have you spoken to her? She might listen to you. I suspect she just tunes out when she hears me these days.'

'I don't know if confrontation will get us anywhere, but I'm around today doing a few bits, so if I see her, I'll try to have a word.'

That was about as good a commitment I could hope for from Nick, so I got my things and headed in for work, glad to be leaving the troubles of the estate behind me.

20

McCann called around later that evening. He looked well turned out in a fresh blue shirt that showed just enough of his well-tanned chest.

'How are we?' he said when I opened the door. He looked past me into the hall, like he was expecting to be invited in.

'*We* are fine,' I replied. 'Busy at the moment with work I have to catch up on. I've had another incident last night, so I missed out on work this morning.'

'Oh?' He looked concerned.

'Yeah, someone put a grass snake through my cat flap and scared the crap out of me.'

'That's strange, and you're sure it wasn't just an escapee snake? You know teens these days, they keep all sorts of things.'

'There aren't too many teens around here, and I suspect it wouldn't have just wandered in. Besides, with the other stuff that has been happening, it seems to fit a pattern.'

He stood back a little. 'I wouldn't jump to conclusions, June. It could be just a bad run.'

'With the killing of Fred as well? Is that part of a bad run?'

'Well, hopefully, there's no connection there at all. That was a dreadful thing. What's happened to you is very unpleasant, but I don't think there's any comparison.'

'I'm not saying there's a comparison, but there seems to be a pattern in what's happening.' I was starting to get irritated with him because he was downplaying what had happened to me. He stood back some more in the doorway and looked very serious. It was clear things were not going the way he had hoped.

'June, you need to have a night off. I think things are getting to you, and who could blame you? What happened to Fred was simply awful, and it really must have had a strong psychological impact.'

That annoyed me even more. It was like he was making out I was some doddery old woman who was losing her marbles. 'Maybe you're right. A night off would be just the thing, if I can put up with someone targeting my house for what reason I don't know and with two grown-up children who seem to think I am public enemy number one these days. I'm going to go in now and pour myself a glass of wine.'

I closed the door on him, although I could see him lurch forward just before I did, as if he was going to try to stop me.

Sitting in an armchair with Tammy on the sofa and a glass of red in my hands, it took me a full five minutes to wind down from that encounter. Had I been over the top with him? I didn't think so. He really had been downplaying what had happened to me and made it seem like I was losing my marbles. Besides, I was still left with a very uneasy feeling after what he had said about Fred's photos. I'd be giving McCann a wide berth until all this was sorted. No doubt, I was attracted to him with his suave good looks, but this was a time when I had to keep my cards close to my chest and find out exactly what was going on before I could trust anyone.

'I need money for a field trip in college. We're going doing some outdoor adventure thing. It's two hundred.' That was Sam's greeting when he came in. I nodded vaguely, too tired to question further. Money was always an issue. Even though I was good with it, bills quietly piled up, and each month was a struggle. Nick was supposed to pay regular maintenance, but as often as not, he'd have some excuse and give something short of what he was supposed to. I had become weary of wrangling with him and definitely wasn't going to sour things even more between all of us by bringing it to the courts.

I will ask him for a hundred of this, though, for Sam, I thought.

Later that night, I went to the emergency stash of cash I kept in a drawer upstairs. I always had five hundred just in case and hadn't dipped into it in a long time, but when I went to get it, I saw there was only two hundred and fifty there. That caused me to sit on my bed and run through the last time I had taken from it. It was around Christmas as far as I could remember, and I was sure I had topped it back up again.

My first thought was Sam and the weed habit he seemed to have developed. Would he go so far as to steal money? Not the Sam I knew, but I thought about how you heard young people changing as they smoked more, particularly with the strong weed going around. I knew from my own work that a lot of addiction referrals were now coming in for weed. *Oh, God,* I thought, *if it is that, how am I going to approach him? If I ask, then I am more or less accusing him.*

Then I wondered about Cathy. She had fallen under Steve's spell, and he was someone I knew had a criminal history. Was it possible that he had persuaded her, for whatever reason? Again, that wasn't like the Cathy I knew, but she had changed since she got involved with Steve.

The only other person with access to the house was Nick,

but I really couldn't see him stooping that low. I would have to broach it with Sam and Cathy in as subtle a way as I could.

I got my chance with Sam later on. He was just back in from Philly's.

'That sounds nice, going on an outdoorsy adventure with the college.'

'Yeah, we have to do a write-up on it,' he replied sullenly. 'Goes towards our end-of-year mark.'

'Well, at least it's something concrete to write about.'

He didn't reply to that, having busied himself with a glass of milk and a couple of oat cookies.

'Do you know what? I think I'm going scatty and forgetful in my old age. I've misplaced some money I usually have around.'

I deliberately left a pause after saying that to gauge his reaction, but he kept his attention on the milk and cookies, dunking the cookies slowly in and then sucking the milk through them. He looked for all the world like a child, trans-fixed on his little world.

'But don't worry, I'll have the money for the trip tomorrow.'

'Thanks.' He looked up briefly as he said it and then went back to the world of milk and cookies. That made me think that he couldn't possibly have anything to do with it unless he had suddenly turned into a master actor.

He headed for bed shortly after. I stayed up because I was hoping Cathy would be in. I didn't want to seem casual about her staying out, especially if it involved Steve. I was trying to formulate a way I could run the money question by her when she breezed in.

'I'm just getting a couple of things,' she said hurriedly. I could put the rest of the sentence together myself without her telling me. She was going to be staying at Steve's, and that was why she needed her 'couple of things'. There was absolutely no point in trying to say anything about the money. Cathy was rushing, and the situation was already tense.

'Are you coming back tonight?'

'Maybe.'

'Cathy, you are coming to the end of the college year. You need to get sleep and get in for the morning lectures.'

Cathy put her hands on her hips. Her overnight bag was at her feet. 'I know what I'm doing, Mam. I got this far on my own steam, didn't I?'

Cathy had actually done well in college to date. She had been interested and engaged and had a good capacity for critical thinking, all of which had been reflected in her marks. I couldn't deny that, but she seemed at risk of blowing it all.

'I know you did, and I've told you how proud I am of what you did, but this isn't a time to start slacking.'

'I'm not slacking. I just have a couple of assignments to get in. Besides, Steve is so busy we need to take whatever opportunity we can get.'

He didn't look 'so busy' to me, standing around in his driveway with his cars, music blaring, but I wasn't going to say that. Any attack on Steve would be seen as an attack on her or evidence of my snobbery.

'Just be careful. You have a lot to lose.' I didn't know what else to say, and I didn't want her to go on a bad note. I could see she was going anyway unless we had a big fight over it, and I didn't feel that would get us anywhere.

'Good night, Mam.' Cathy picked up her bag and left.

I GOT a chance to talk to Nick the next day after work. Steve was out in his drive as I got back, music blaring, grinning over at me. I took a deep breath and went into the house. Nick arrived about a half hour after me. I had texted him and said

we needed to talk. I wasn't going to confront him about the
money, of course, but I felt I could sound him out. More than
that, I wanted to see if he had anything further to say about
Steve and Cathy. She was clearly in danger of blowing her
college altogether.

'Well?' He plodded in the door with the look of someone
who has put in a hard day's work, overalls grassy and hands
still mucky. He washed his hands before putting the kettle on
and joining me at the table with a mug of tea and some of his
never-ending stash of biscuits.

'I needed to ask you for money for Sam. He's going on an
outdoor adventure trip, part of some assignment. He needs
two hundred, so whatever you can contribute.'

Nick looked out the window in response. His brow was
furrowed. 'Of course. When does he need it?' he said eventually in a ponderous voice.

'Tomorrow, I think. I can cover it for the moment, so you
can give it back to me.'

Nick smiled without warmth. 'Sure. It's just I'm waiting on
a pay-out from McCann. He's going to come up with it
shortly, just some cash-flow issues, but it'll be a good chunk
when I get it.'

That sent alarm bells ringing. He was waiting on cash
from McCann, so he was obviously short. Someone in that
situation might just decide they would take an unofficial
'loan'.

'Oh. You've been working for him for a while now. Surely,
he can give you part payment.' I was suspicious with Nick,
but at the same time, if he was getting the run-around from
McCann, that wasn't on.

Nick stiffened. 'So you think maybe he has paid me some,
but I'm holding back?'

'No, that's not what I meant. I think it's very unfair of him not to have paid you at all. How are you supposed to keep going?'

'He'll be good for it. Some businessmen operate like that. They prefer to pay people in lumps rather than in bits and pieces.'

I wasn't convinced. McCann had too much of the smooth salesman about him, and Nick, for all his other faults, was a bit of an innocent when it came to other people.

'It's okay. I'll cover Sam for the moment, but there were a couple of other things I wanted to ask you about. First was if you think Sam is smoking a lot of weed. He's spending lots of time with that guy Philly, and he seems to come home stoned.'

'Is he getting his college work done?'

'He seems to be scraping by. That won't be enough to get him the scholarship for next year. They look at both academic and sports performance.'

'Hmm. I'll have a word with him. He just needs to put on an extra spurt for the end of the year.'

'Then, I'm not sure how to say this, but some money went missing, and I was wondering if Sam could have taken it to pay for weed.'

Nick shook his head vigorously. 'Not Sam. He was always an honest kid.'

'Then who?'

Nick pursed his lips. 'Could it have just fallen out and be stuck behind a drawer?'

'Doubt it. I had a good look.'

Nick furrowed his brow again. 'Surely, not Cathy.'

'I don't know. I really don't, but that brings me to the next question. Have you spoken to her? She was with Steve again last night.'

'I honestly haven't had a chance. I'll put it top of my agenda, though.'

'It may be too late by the time you get to that agenda. She seems very serious about her relationship, and I, for one, am very worried.'

'It's a worry, all right,' Nick said distractedly.

I got no sense of commitment from Nick and was tired of trying to tease any out of him. He finished his tea and left, promising that he would talk to Cathy at the first available opportunity. I felt that opportunity might have been a long way off. That night, as I thought about it all, I felt very alone. There was nobody there to support me. Nick was, as usual, preoccupied with his own life. My two kids were immersed in their own worlds. There had been no news from the Gardai on the killing of Fred. I had seen the detectives around the estate, so they were obviously still following up on leads, but whoever did it was still out there, and that was a very worrying thought.

FRED'S FUNERAL took place the next day. The coroner had finally released the body after the post-mortem had been completed. The service took place in a small church about a mile from the house. There were just a few people there, with Cathal and what I took to be an aunt and uncle standing in the front pew.

Cathy and Sam were with me, and I was glad to have them on either side. Jim McCann showed up, as did a very shaky Paul, and then, to my surprise, Steve walked in. To my even greater surprise, he came to sit beside Cathy in our pew. I felt myself instinctively pull away when he slid in, but he smiled across Cathy at me and shook his head before nodding towards Fred's coffin.

Mercifully, the priest appeared and started speaking.

'We are here to celebrate the life and mark the unfortunate death of Fred Summers.' He went through some introductory prayers before gesturing towards Cathal. 'I will now call on his son, Cathal, to say a few words.'

I saw Cathal move shakily towards the altar and the microphone. He had some crumpled sheets of paper in his hand, which he flattened on the lectern. Even from where I sat, I could see his hands were shaking. He took a deep breath and looked down at the notes he had flattened.

'My father was a quiet man, a devoted husband and a good father. He lost Margaret, my mother and his wife, far too early, and life for him was never the same after that. But even in his grief, he was there for his family and for his neighbours. He took great pride in his house. That was where all his memories were, so it is so sad that it's where he met such a brutal end.' Cathal paused and lifted his head up to look out at the small congregation. The sorrow of the moment had strained his otherwise youthful face. 'It shouldn't have ended for him like that, but I know that I and the other members of his small family will keep the memory of the kind, caring, considerate man that he was alive, because that is what he would want. My dad would never harm anyone, and he would never wish harm on anyone. I hope the person who did this realizes what they have done, taken a caring man away from us in such a terrible way, but we will do our best to preserve the memory of the good man we knew.'

There was a heavy silence in the church after he finished those last words, a silence that was only broken by the poignant sound of Cathal gathering his notes up again and unsteadily making his way back to his pew.

The priest continued with the funeral mass until he walked down the aisle, in front of the coffin, waving his incense censer from side to side. Cathal and the small family group walked immediately behind the coffin, arms linked for support.

We all followed them out and stood around the back of the hearse. Sam and Cathy both went over to Cathal to offer condolences. McCann hovered at the edges of the group, looking over at the mourners and shaking his head wistfully.

Steve, to my horror, came to stand beside me.

'It's terrible, isn't it? He must have been a good guy.'

I wasn't sure how to react. My first instinct was to just move away, but there was nowhere to go.

'Yes, he was a good man,' I replied curtly. Steve didn't respond to that, but I saw McCann move over beside us.

'Such a shame,' he said, shaking his head.

'Yes, it's awful,' I replied. I was about to leave the two of them standing there when Nick came at a run right up to us. He was panting and sweating.

'God, I missed it, didn't I?'

'Well, you missed the church part, but there's still the burial to go.'

Nick checked his watch and looked at McCann. 'I've too much on. Those gardens don't stop growing.'

'Take your time,' McCann said. 'He was your neighbour for some years.'

'I know, but there's so few people here. It would look ridiculous, me at the graveside. I'll just say a few words to Cathal.'

He bustled through the small throng to get to Cathal. McCann watched with an air of detachment. For my part, I wondered at Nick's fawning attitude towards McCann and couldn't resist saying what came out next.

'Nick seems very busy, all right. It'll be all worth it, I suppose, when he gets paid.'

McCann's expression turned darker. His boyish good looks disappeared completely, and it was like a chilling, ruthless version of himself stepped into his shoes, but he regathered quickly, and the darkness evaporated as quickly as it had appeared. He gestured at the funeral group.

'This is hardly the time to discuss business matters, is it?'

'No, but that's not really business, is it? Paying someone is what's expected for the work they do.'

His expression darkened again. I could see he was struggling to keep it in check.

'You have a habit of pushing yourself in where you don't belong. That's a risky strategy in life, I have found.'

'I'm looking after my own interests. Nick and I have an agreement, and he has to keep his side of it.'

'I would say look after your own end, and he will look after his.'

Nick came bustling back towards us at that point. I could see relief on his face. 'They're not expecting anyone outside of immediate family to go to the graveside. He's getting buried quite far away in some scenic place outside the city. That's where Margaret is.'

I broke away from our little group then and went over to Cathal. McCann was glaring at me, and I could feel his eyes follow me all the way over. Sam and Cathy were still with Cathal.

'If there's anything we can do, let us know,' I said to him. 'Stay in touch with us, anyway.'

'Thanks, but I'm not sure when I'll be back again. This is going to take a long time to get over.'

I gave him a quick hug, and the three of us left. I was glad to get back in the car and drive away. The little scene with Nick, Steve and McCann had been unsettling. Nick seemed so tied in with McCann. He was now almost completely dependent on him, yet McCann wasn't in any hurry to pay him. *Maybe that's exactly where he wants him*, I thought. Nick was a malleable character, anyway. He tried to present the outward appearance of strength and certainty, but once you got to know him, all that started to crumble away. Behind that façade lay someone who was happy to retreat into selfishness and would do anything to serve his own needs. My feeling was that McCann had spotted that and was enjoying the power he held over him. But to what end? What was McCann's goal?

Then where did Steve fit into the picture? The fact that he wanted to be beside us at the funeral. Well, of course, he was now involved with Cathy, but did he need to be at the funeral at all? He hardly knew Fred, and I was pretty sure what he did know of him, he didn't like. Fred certainly had no time for him. So was he using us as some sort of cover to gain respectability in the eyes of the world? Worse still, was he using us to cover up something terrible he had done?

I didn't like the position he was putting us in one little bit. I was going to have to do what I could to figure out what was going on. The attacks on my own house seemed like they were building towards something. Was Steve involved in those? He seemed like the most likely culprit, and he had the criminal past to back it up. But what was McCann up to with Nick, and were the two things connected? Did Steve and McCann have something going on? The possibilities seemed endless.

21

Next day, I was back after lunch to do some work from home. There were a couple of cars outside Fred's house. I assumed at first that it was the detectives, but I saw the couple come out who had asked me if I wanted to sell my house. With them was Cathal, Fred's son. They chatted for a while, and then the couple headed off in their car. I saw Cathal going in and out of the house, so I went out to him.

'You doing something with the house?' I asked when he had paused to check his phone in the driveway.

He looked up and nodded. 'Yes, I'm selling it. I was humming and hawing as to what to do when I got a call from that couple. They made a decent offer, and it was too hard to resist.'

'Oh, that's good.' I didn't know what to say. My immediate reaction was a deep unease. How did that all happen so fast?

'Yes, it is. I mean, it's the family home, and it really isn't easy doing this, but in a way, I have no choice. I'm all the way over in Canada, and I can't be coming back and forth. I have my life over there now. When the offer came in, I had to think long and hard about it, but they have all the finances ready, so I just took the plunge.'

My sense of unease deepened. Who were these people, and how did they know to move so quickly?

'If you need a hand with anything, let me know.' That was all I could think of saying.

'Thanks, but I'm okay. I have a solicitor working on the sale, and then all I've got to do is get the place cleared. I should be able to fly back home in a couple of days.'

He went back to his phone, and I went back inside. Having new neighbours so soon was something I certainly hadn't bargained for, and that couple had made me uneasy from the first time I saw them. Still, there was nothing I could do about it. Cathal had obviously made his mind up about it, and I had nothing concrete on the couple, just a sense that there was something off about them.

That sense increased a couple of days later. The couple were in and out of the house. I could see removal men taking all of Fred's stuff away. Cathal was there for a bit too. Towards evening, things had quietened down, but the couple were still around. I felt it was a good time to talk to them and try to put my fears about them to rest, so I went out to fuss around my garden and called over to Stephanie when I saw her come out.

'Everything okay?' I asked. 'Must be a heck of a lot of clearing out to do.'

Stephanie stopped to consider me and the remark I had made. She looked different from the day she had called in to me. She was wearing jeans and a T-shirt and had a slew of earrings in one ear. I could see a couple of tattoos on the arm nearest to me. Her look, when her eyes met mine, was more of a sizing up than anything else.

'Bit to do, all right, but we'll get through it. He kept the place in good nick, anyway.'

I didn't like the way she talked about Fred as a 'he', and she seemed to view the house just as a commodity.

'Yes, he was very house proud. Everything that Fred did, he liked to do it right.'

'So it seems.' Stephanie took her phone out to check it. She looked back at me as if to check whether I was still there.

'So will you be moving in soon?'

'Us? Oh no, that's not the plan. This place is going to be rented. We just have to get it in order first. Still a bit of paperwork to come through, but we'll have it sorted soon.' She checked her phone again, then looked at me, nodded, and continued down the drive towards her car.

I went back inside and sat in an armchair. I had to take in what she had just told me because the feeling that something was 'off' about the couple had just gone through the roof. Thinking back to the time they had called in to me looking to buy my house, they had gone on about how much they liked the area and how they'd love to live here. Now that they had bought Fred's house next door, they seemed to have no intention of living here. So why had they gone on about it so much the first time? The only reason I could think of was that they were trying to fool me. But why would they go to such lengths to do it? Why did they so desperately want to get their hands on either my house or Fred's?

I decided someone who might have some answers would be Jim McCann. He was in the rental business. Maybe he could see an angle that I didn't. I didn't particularly want to talk to him, but if anyone could shed any light on it, he could.

I got my chance later on that evening as I spotted him sitting in his car outside Philly's house. I went innocently to work in my front garden, pretending not to notice he was there. He took the bait and jumped out a couple of minutes later.

'You're doing the right thing, June,' he said cheerily. 'It's the best way to unwind after a day's work, get out in the garden and relax.'

I didn't see him as someone who would do much gardening, but I kept my powder dry.

'Yes, you're right. There's something about the garden that just puts you in relax mode. It must be the quiet hum of nature going on that settles us.'

'Too right, June. We've become too automated, spend too much of our time on screens. That takes us away from what really matters.'

I wondered what really mattered for him. He never gave much away, but he was all full of charm and inoffensive remarks. The real Jim McCann stayed hidden from view.

'I see that my neighbour's house has been sold already.' I nodded in the direction of Fred's. I had left the comment deliberately open to see how he would react.

'So I heard. I saw a bit of activity around the place, so I made my enquiries.'

'It was a couple who had come asking about my house a while back.'

'Oh, yes?' McCann had his eyebrows raised.

'Yeah. They said how much they wanted to settle here, but now I hear they are going to rent it.'

'Good rental market around here, as I said before.'

He must know more about this than he's saying, I thought. *This is his bread and butter, yet he's making out he only knows as much as me.*

'You missed a chance to get in there?'

'Not necessarily. I may actually end up working with them on the rental bit.'

'Oh, so you've had some contact?'

'Well, an indirect sort of thing.'

'You like to keep your cards close to your chest, don't you?'

McCann looked sharply up at me.

He didn't like that question, I thought. I had made it deliberately provocative to try to get a reaction.

'I'm pretty good at my business, June. Sometimes too good. People say I should give more of my life to other things, but I get obsessed. I like to stay on top of things. Some might even call me a control freak, but I wouldn't put it that way. Things weren't always so good, and I remember those times. Does that answer your question?' He had a hint of his old charming smile back, but it looked forced.

'I suppose it does. Now, I don't want to keep you from that business you like to keep on top of.' I turned and started walking away.

'No fear of that, June. Hope I didn't come across too serious there, but the past stays with us, doesn't it?'

I didn't have an answer for that question, and to be honest, I wasn't sure what he was talking about. I felt relieved but none the wiser when I closed the door behind me. He had seemed defensive about Fred's house or like he had something to hide. *Maybe it's just down to machismo, losing out on a good deal and me calling him out on it,* I thought.

I spent some time thinking it all through with a cup of tea and Tammy beside me on the sofa. The nagging thought of McCann commenting about Fred's photos stayed with me as I thought it all through. He seemed to have had at least an interest in Fred's house, so why would he be so oblivious to someone else buying it under his nose? Maybe it was just done so quickly he didn't have time to react. Nothing added up. The couple, who had seemed strange from the get-go, buying their dream home and then immediately putting it up for rent. That made no sense at all unless they were being duplicitous from the start. There seemed to be too many actors involved in our little estate, and they were all pursuing some agenda that was baffling to me. It brought me back to what Fred had been trying to say as he died, something

beginning with *B* and with a *B* in the middle. The trouble was
I wasn't sure if it meant anything at all. He had been so badly
injured, he could have just been rambling, but I decided I
would try to look into it. I would start doing my own research.
I had already looked into Steve's background and found some
very unsavoury information. Maybe it was time I looked into
McCann as well. Did he have something to hide, and if so,
what was it?

22

E vents took over the following day that prevented me from doing research of any kind into McCann. I spent a reasonable day at work, saw a couple of clients and got them out of their crisis situations, then settled in to the mountain of paperwork. In ways, I was glad of the distraction. All the permutations in our estate were just swirling round and round my head, and I seemed to be getting nowhere with them. I focused on the work, glad as well to be making up for the time that I had lost, so I stayed on late and got home well after the traffic had died down.

There were a couple of frozen shepherd's pies in the freezer, so I defrosted them in the microwave, put on a pot of peas, and there I had dinner for whoever was around. I could hear some movement upstairs, so I called up. Cathy gave a muffled response, and twenty minutes later, the two of us were sitting down to dinner. Sam was still away at his outdoor adventure trip.

'How's work?' Cathy asked, and although it shouldn't, the question threw me. I wasn't used to the kids taking an actual interest in my daily life. Generally, the focus was on their needs and how to get them. I was suspicious but decided to take the question at face value, so I launched into an account of the various crises and bureaucratic hoops that comprised my day. Cathy nodded along. She did have an interest in social issues and had been out on a couple of protests, one for homelessness and one around the 'me too' movement.

'And how did college go for you?' I reciprocated when I had finished.

'Yep, grand. Getting through the work.' Cathy fiddled with a bit of food on her plate before looking up. 'Mam, I have a bit of news, and it may not go down too well, but it is something I am very excited about.'

That caused me to stop in mid-bite and pull a forkful of food away from my mouth and back to the plate. The news, I felt, was not going to be good. I could see Cathy take a deep breath and prepare herself to deliver it.

'It's about me and Steve,' she said with an exhalation of breath.

In my book, that was about as bad a start as she could have made. Anything to do with her and Steve was bad news unless it was to do with their breaking up. Somehow, I doubted that was the news she was going to come out with.

'I'm moving in with him.' She said that with another exhalation, then looked up at me for a response. I am not sure what my face looked like, but my innards had reacted by twisting themselves into a knot of tension. I could feel something deep down in my stomach that was rising, and I didn't know whether it was going to be a scream or tears or what. I took a deep breath to try to hold it at bay and counted to ten in my head. Whatever came out, I wanted it to be as close to rational as possible.

'Moving in how?' I asked, although there was only one answer to that question.

'Moving in as in living together. We've talked a lot about

it, and it makes sense. He has the girls, and I could be there a lot for them, and it gives us a bit of stability, you know, that we don't have to keep on making arrangements.'

'Cathy, you only live two houses down from Steve. Why do you think you need to move in?' I was managing to keep calm and was looking for a practical approach.

Cathy dropped her fork on her plate, and its rattle filled the uneasy silence as she prepared her answer. 'We're grown-ups, Mam. We want to be able to live our own lives without asking permission.'

'Nobody expects you to ask permission, but have you thought through the practicality of it? If you move in, then you're going to have to come up with money for food and bills. Where will you get that?'

'Steve said not to worry about any of that for the moment.'

'For the moment? What happens when that changes? And even before it changes, is he going to have a hold over you if you're not contributing?'

Cathy sighed in exasperation. 'He's not like that, Mam. Steve's an incredibly generous person. He doesn't want the petty day-to-day things to get in the way.'

'Cathy, I've been around long enough and gone through enough trouble of my own to know that people change in a relationship, and moving in with someone is a very big step. You should give yourself a couple of weeks to think about it before making a move that big.'

'A couple of weeks?' Cathy's voice had gone up a couple of octaves with exasperation. 'No, Mam, we've already thought it all through. If it doesn't work out, I can always come back, but we want to give it a go.'

That knot started twisting again in my stomach. This was a looming disaster, but I had to try to handle it diplomatically; otherwise there would just be a big blowout, and she would end up storming out.

'It's a huge step, and you have to think about how well you know Steve.'

Cathy smiled at that. 'I know him plenty well. I am able to make character judgements, you know.'

'I know you are, but the age difference is so big as well. That worries me.' There was a host of things that worried me about it, but I was trying to focus on the obvious, practical ones.

'I've made my mind up, Mam, or should I say we've made our minds up? I'm going to start moving my stuff tonight.'

She went upstairs, and I could hear her moving around. I felt helpless in the situation, not knowing what to do but feeling I had to do something. But what?

Just then, there was a knock on the door. I opened it to find a grinning Steve standing outside.

'Is Cathy here?' he asked through the grin.

'She's upstairs. I have to tell you I'm not happy about this move. Cathy is way too young. It's just too big a step for her. You should be able to guide her better. You know how impetuous younger people are. You've already had a relationship that didn't work out, so you know how it can go wrong.'

The grin disappeared in a flash and was replaced by a jutting chin and gritted teeth.

'My past relationships have nothing to do with you.'

'I know that, but I am talking about your experience, something that Cathy has very little of.'

'Well, she's about to get some, isn't she? We live and learn, as they say.' He gave me a leery smile after saying that, like he was challenging me. I wanted to shout at him at the top of my lungs, but I held back.

'As I said before, she might even want to start a family. Better start when you're young, don't you think?'

'That's not what I want for my daughter. You know that quite well. She still has to finish college.'

'The university of life, June. That's where we do the real learning.'

Cathy came struggling down the stairs with a suitcase in one hand and a bag over her shoulder. Steve made as if to go in and help her, but I stood in front of him. No way was he getting in my house. He shrugged at my gesture, then leaned an arm in to grab the suitcase.

Cathy bustled past me. She turned and smiled as she did. 'I've a couple more things to collect, so I'll be back in a bit.'

Steve leered at me again. 'Sure. We're not far, anyway. You can drop in any time you like, June.'

I saw Cathy throw him a dirty look; then she continued on out the door. At that moment, Nick pulled up in the pickup. I could see him sitting looking out, sizing up the situation. He saw me eyeballing him, so he stepped quickly out and walked up the drive.

'What's going on?' he asked to no one in particular.

'Cathy is moving in with Steve,' I replied, keeping it as simple and succinct as possible.

'Oh, so soon?' He ran his hand through his thinning hair.

'It felt right, Dad, so we're going ahead with it. No point in waiting around.'

'But college?' Nick spread his arms as if in exasperation, but his tone was watery.

'Yeah, college will keep going.' Cathy started lugging her bag down the drive. Steve pulled her suitcase after her. The suitcase wobbled unsteadily on small plastic wheels. It nearly toppled over, but Steve grabbed it in time.

'She must have stuffed the whole house in this thing,' Steve said with a smile.

Nick laughed, then he looked at me, and his expression turned serious again. 'It's all a bit premature,' he said weakly.

Steve ignored him and kept going. Nick looked at me and shrugged. I was too upset to say anything, so I turned around and went back inside. Nick followed me in.

'There's nothing we can do, is there?'

'It's a bit late now, isn't it? Cathy has made her mind up. Did you ever get to talk to her?'

'No, but I will. She'll see that things aren't as rosy as she thinks once they settle in.'

'Might be too late by then.'

Nick had no answer for that. He put the kettle on.

'I'll have tea as well,' I said as I saw him fill just one mug.

'Of course.' When the tea was made and he sat at the table, he looked out the window towards Steve's house. 'It might work out, you know. Steve's not a bad guy. I've got to know him a bit from being around.'

'Maybe he is, and maybe he isn't, but this is not a good time for our daughter to be taking big chances like this. Don't forget we still have an unsolved murder on our estate.'

Nick stiffened at that remark and stared glumly into his tea. 'Yes, of course. Poor Fred.'

23

C athy was back in later that evening to get some more of her things. She hurried about her business, probably nervous that I was going to try to stop her altogether, but I had resigned myself to the situation for the moment. She was clearly intent on going. We could have a massive row, and she would just end up going anyway, so I said nothing.

She paused before going out the front door and turned back in to stand near me where I was sitting.

'It'll be okay, Mam. I promise.'

I smiled at her because I had no response to that. I didn't think it was okay, and I didn't think it would turn out well, but she had made her decision. I spent the rest of the evening listening to music on the radio. There was a DJ I liked who played a good mix of jazz and world music, so I settled in to lose myself in that. I started thinking about what Nick had said. The comment on 'poor Fred' seemed like such an understatement. It was like he saw it as some unfortunate incident that had happened in the past and we had moved on. I felt very differently about it. Fred was a friend and a neighbour. His death was horrible. Nothing like that should happen to anyone, let alone a kindly gent who minded his own business.

I knew the detectives were still working on it, but progress seemed to be slow. I hadn't heard of anyone being brought in for a second round of questioning yet. Maybe they were still going through the forensics before they made a move. I decided I had to do something, and my starting point was the only clue I had—the word that Fred had been trying to say before he died.

I slept an uneasy sleep, but when I woke in the morning, I felt galvanized. No way was I going to sit back and just let events take their course. I was going to do what I could to help solve Fred's death.

The word Fred had been trying to say before he died was something with a couple of Bs in it. I knew it might only be the ramblings of someone who was losing consciousness, but something about the determination with which he had tried to say it made me feel it was more than that. There was nobody with a name like that I could think of, so if he was trying to say someone's name, then it must have been some-body from outside, and I would have no chance at all of figuring that out. The other option was that it wasn't a person's name at all but something connected with the house or the estate.

I toyed with the word all day. Whenever I had a pause in work or stopped for a coffee, I let the B sound roll around in my head. I even wrote it down a couple of times like B... B... Finally, towards the end of my working day, I could feel some-thing start to break through. It was a feeling at first, but it soon became something more tangible. I remembered the name of the property company who had put in for planning permission to build a massive block of student accommoda-tion right behind me and Fred. That company had started with a *B*. I couldn't remember exactly what the name was, but it was 'br', I was pretty sure, and had another *B* somewhere in the middle. I started Googling, playing around with *B*s at the start of the names of companies who had been involved in building, and finally, after trying lots of variations, I spotted a name that suddenly looked all too familiar—Brabazon Holdings.

Once I saw it, the whole scenario came flooding back to me. They had put in the planning application but had stayed way in the background and had let a solicitor firm do the brunt of the housework. Our objection to the planning application had been sustained. At the time, it made sense to me that Brabazon Holdings had stayed in the background. If they'd tried to contact us directly, it might prejudice the outcome of the application. I had taken the proceedings at face value, and when our objection won the day, I had thought no more about it. Now, I wondered, could that possibly be the word that Fred was trying to say? It seemed far-fetched that would actually be the case, but it was the only lead I had. Besides, I was a believer in the power of intuition, and something about the way that revelation had slowly dawned on me had felt right. It was definitely worth looking into. But first, I had to find out who they were, and that proved a little more difficult.

I went home and started digging through everything I could find from the time of the application. I had kept files during the case, and mercifully, I still had them. I had been afraid that Brabazon would appeal the decision to block the ruling against them. They had done exactly that. The appeal had gone nowhere, but still, being the cautious person that I am, I kept all the information.

Rooting through the files, I found the name of the solicitor we had dealt with. I would call them first thing in the morning and see what they could tell me. Meanwhile, I

checked online for Brabazon Holdings and saw that they
were no longer registered as a company. Their termination
date was set somewhere just after the attempt to gain planning permission. That sent up a red flag immediately. If
they'd folded straight after an application like that and
seemed to have little history in the building trade, then what
were they? I would have to wait till morning to get any type of
answer.

Sam came back from the outdoor adventure later in the
evening. He carried a filthy sports bag that he threw beside
the washing machine in the kitchen and plonked himself
wearily on a chair, running his hand through his mop of
curls.

'Have a good trip?' I was deliberately not noticing the
demonstrative display of nonverbals.

'Knackered,' was all he could manage to respond with.

'Tiring, then?'

'Yeah, they made us sleep under bivouacs, like little
plastic strips on a branch, and then we had to sleep on the
ground with, like, something as thin as a yoga mat
underneath.'

'Sounds tough.' I walked over to him and rubbed a hand
on his shoulder. He flinched initially but settled down then
and let me rub.

'Here, let me fix you some hot food and a mug of tea, then
you can run a bath, okay?' He nodded faintly to that suggestion, so I set about getting the remains of a curry heated for
him and slid a mug of steaming tea under his nose. He sipped
tentatively from the tea, like someone who has been out of
civilization for so long they hardly remember what it tastes
like. The curry followed swiftly, and he attacked that with a
more familiar purpose until the plate was empty of every
morsel.

'Have a bit of news,' I said once his posture had relaxed.

'Yeah?' He looked up at me, and I think it was the first eye contact we made since he got back.

'Yes, Cathy has moved in with Steve. She took her things across last night.'

'She what?' His mouth dropped open a couple of inches in genuine shock.

'Moved in with Steve.'

'With him?' Sam kept up the look of shock. I was a little surprised because he'd normally be sticking up for Cathy no matter what. It was probably because he was so tired, he had his guard down, but I was glad to see it. Sam obviously thought it was a bad idea too.

'Yes, nothing I could say would stop her.'

Sam shrugged. He composed himself and dropped the look of shock. 'It'll probably turn out okay. Cathy knows what she's doing.'

'I wonder.' I left it at that because it wasn't Sam's problem. 'Anyway, I'll run the bath for you, and you can get yourself a good night's sleep.'

I slept well myself that night. There was a sense of purpose now that I knew what I had to follow up next day. I did keep a half eye on Steve's house and wondered if Cathy might pop over, but there was no sign, so I had a shower, read for a little, and drifted into a sound sleep.

Next morning, first chance I got, I rang the solicitors. Yes, they did remember me and the case, and they had files going back, but due to client confidentiality, they were able to tell me very little except that the company had folded. I knew that already, so I was disappointed with the lack of progress.

I mulled it over during the morning. If the solicitors weren't going to give me any information on Brabazon Holdings, was there anywhere else I could go looking? That thought preoccupied me up to lunchtime. I was getting nowhere with it until I had a thought that should have been obvious to me earlier. Paul, my neighbour, had worked as a freelance architect until his drinking had started getting the better of him. Now he took on odd jobs, but he struggled to make a living with it. However, he still had connections. He might just have some contacts or know where to go looking.

I called into him straight after work. He invited me into his musty, run-down house. Everything smelt old and dusty inside. I hadn't been in for years. Paul kept very much to himself. It was widely known that he had an out-of-control drinking habit, which he tried to manage as discreetly as he could. Part of that management was staying away from people as much as he could.

He presented me with a mug of tea, and we sat in armchairs that faced each other. I had a view towards the street, but it was occluded by a set of blinds that were left open just enough to let the minimum of light in.

'I've been thinking about Fred and the way that he died, and trying to get some answers for myself. When I went in and discovered him on the ground, he was dying, but before he did, he seemed to be saying a word that had a couple of *B*s in it. Now, it mightn't be a clue at all, but I've been racking my brains trying to come up with something. The only thing I can think of is that company, Brabazon Holdings, that applied for the massive student accommodation block behind me and Fred. I checked them out, and they folded straight after their application failed. That makes me wonder what type of company they were. I've tried the solicitors who handled their case, but they won't tell me anything.'

Paul was peering at me through the gloomy light. He was a slight man with thinning hair and round, silver-framed glasses. With his gaunt face, he had the look of a professor or artist who had fallen on hard times.

'It was Steve did it,' he blurted out.

'Oh. How do you know?' I was taken aback by the suddenness and directness of his statement.

'He's nothing but an animal, that guy.'

I could see him grip the sides of his chair with anger.

'He's a dodgy character all right, but is there any evidence?'

'He's next door to Fred, and he's a brute. What more evidence do you need?'

'I think we need to let the police handle that. They'll know what to look for.'

'Bloody useless so far, if you ask me.'

'It's slow, all right, but that's often the way. They need to be sure before they make a move.' I was on the cusp of abandoning my plan. Paul was obviously so worked up about Steve and what had happened. I was afraid he might even take it on himself to do something stupid. I thought maybe I should have just left him be.

'I'll see what I can dig up about that Brabazon Holdings crowd,' he said suddenly. 'I don't think it'll get you anywhere, though.'

'Thanks, Paul. That's very kind of you. Everything is worth trying, I suppose.'

'That was awful what happened to Fred. Nobody deserves that. Nobody.'

I could see his anger rising again. I guessed it was tainted with fear. He was alone in the house, and the drink couldn't always block the fear out.

'It was awful, and that's why we should do anything we can to help.'

'I'll get back to you soon,' he said with finality.

24

There was no word from Paul the next day. I wondered whether I would hear from him at all. His life seemed so erratic, marred by instability. I didn't know him that well, but apparently, he'd had quite a reputation as an architect. He'd had an office in town and even employed a couple of people. That had slid slowly from his grasp. A woman he was engaged to broke off with him, and then he was left in his house, working on scraps and drinking heavily. I put him out of my mind and felt that if he did get back and had some worthwhile information, then that would be a sign I was on the right track.

Meanwhile, I had other concerns to deal with. Steve was out next evening working on his cars, music booming around the street. He threw me a cheeky grin and a wink as I walked from my car to the house. I ignored it, too tired to respond in any way.

When I went in, Cathy was in the kitchen, fixing herself a toasted sandwich. *Didn't take long for her to come back to the home comforts*, I thought.

'Hi, Mam,' she said as she heaved the toasty out, taking

care to keep all the melted cheese inside as she hoisted it onto a plate. She shook her hands after the operation and smiled. 'That melted cheese is pretty hot.'

'So how's things?' I asked in as cheery a tone as I could.

'Yeah, good,' she replied, licking a stray bit of cheese off her fingers. 'Got a good bit of college work done in the last couple of days.'

In the last couple of days, I echoed to myself, *as in she is telling me she works well at Steve's.*

'That's great news. The final push to the end.'

I heated up some soup from a carton for myself and cut a couple of slices of sourdough bread. I wasn't bothered making a dinner.

'Yeah, living with Steve is really working out,' she said as she sat at the table.

'That's good, but it's only two days in.'

'Yeah, but you know the way you get a feel for something.'

I could have told her I had very similar feelings when I moved in with Nick, but that didn't exactly work out.

'Sure, but caution is the order of the day. Take things one step at a time.' I said that even though I was sincerely hoping there would be only one step and then that would be the end of it.

Cathy laughed quietly at that. 'Well, that's kind of something I wanted to talk to you about.'

'What's that?'

'The one step at a time. We have taken the first step, and now maybe it's time to take the second.'

'Like what?' My tone was definitely getting more clipped. Alarm bells were starting to ring very loudly.

Cathy smiled again, like she had some sort of private joke going on. 'Remember the money that Gran left us?'

'The money that you are getting when you're twenty-one?'

'Yeah. That. I was wondering if there was any way that

could be accessed a bit earlier. Like, I am twenty-one in a few months.'

'No. I felt at the time that even twenty-one was a bit young, but your gran had already gone and done it.'

'Well, it was her money too, so it didn't have much to do with what you thought, I suppose.'

I didn't like the tone of her voice and the way she was talking about the inheritance she and Sam had been left by my mother. It was 15,000 each and supposed to be used to pick up any later college bills. I felt I had a strong interest there, as I had been struggling, certainly with Cathy's fees.

'It's supposed to be for post-grad or to set up once you leave home.'

'Well, I have left home, haven't I?'

Cathy was looking at me defiantly. I had to work hard to keep my cool.

'The money is in trust till you are twenty-one.'

'Steve is setting up a proper mechanic's business. He needs some money. He'll have the best business up and running in no time, and then I'll have the money back with interest.'

'You don't know that for sure. It's best to be cautious. It's only a few months till you are able to get it.' I didn't mention that it was something we'd be negotiating anyway as to how it was spent.

'Mum, it's my money. I can do what I want with it.'

'When you are twenty-one.'

'It's because of Steve, isn't it? You still have that prejudice. That's pure snobbery, Mum. You need to get over yourself.' With that, Cathy rushed from the table to throw her dishes in the sink and then dash back out the door. I had to take a few deep breaths to calm down again. I could feel myself trembling with tension.

That's Steve putting her up to it, I thought, *trying to squeeze whatever he can out of her.*

That suspicion was confirmed later on that evening. I was out trying to relax by tending my garden. I had seen Steve heading off with his snarling dogs, so I knew the coast was clear to get a bit of work done. I felt nostalgic as I potted around outside for the days when I could see the front garden as a real sanctuary. I was enjoying tidying up my flower beds and listening to the quiet hum of bees as they sought out the sweetest nectar when I heard the sound of the panting dogs approaching. Steve had taken a very short walk and was bearing down on me with that taunting grin of his.

'Doing a bit in the garden, I see,' he said as he approached.

I must have unconsciously backed off when I saw the two brutish dogs straining at their leashes, their heads switching from side to side as they pulled in what looked like a frantic bid to escape.

'Don't mind these lads. They're pussycats.'

I did mind 'these lads' and backed off a couple more steps.

'Cathy tells me you're keeping a tight grip on the purse strings.'

'That's none of your business.'

'It's all my business now, isn't it? We're setting up a life together, aren't we? Share and share alike.'

'What are you sharing?' I asked and immediately regretted it.

Steve's taunting grin grew even wider. 'Me? I'm sharing everything, if you know what I mean.'

'Cathy doesn't get that money till she's twenty-one,' I said, bringing the conversation back to the factual.

'Well, that's not too far away, is it? Good times ahead.' He let the dogs pull him off towards his house as he gave a last goading smile in my direction.

I went back inside when he left. The joy of working in the garden had receded. It felt like Steve was invading my privacy from every possible angle. I was very worried about what kind of conversations Cathy might be having with him. If she told him about the inheritance she was due, then what else was she telling him? I imagined that all my private life and our family's business were being laid bare to somebody who would use it for his own purposes whenever he liked. Cathy might well have been trying to impress him by talking about the money, and as soon as he heard it, he realized he could exploit that vulnerability. He was so streetwise, and Cathy was so innocent. The worst thing was she thought she was streetwise just because she had enormous empathy for anyone who was struggling. I could have easily imagined Steve manipulating that empathy. The longer she stayed with him, the more likely he was to exploit her. The more I thought about it, the more I got into a panic.

As I dwelt on it, I couldn't help thinking of what Paul had said when I spoke about Fred's murder. He had no doubt it was Steve who did it. While I understood he had a grudge against Steve, when I thought about who might have killed Fred myself, it was very easy to imagine Steve as a killer. He had that ability to switch from warm and charming to ice-cold and dangerous in a split second. Had there been some sort of interaction between him and Fred that I didn't know about? That was quite likely, as Fred was so upset by having such a thug as a neighbour.

It led me to think about the strange things that had been happening to me as well. Someone was definitely targeting my house with the bin fire, the car alarm and the snake. Then the money that was missing from the emergency stash. Was there any connection between that and the other things that had happened? I sincerely hoped not because if there was, that meant either someone had broken into my house or that someone inside the house was in some way involved. But if they were, why would Cathy, Sam or Nick get involved in a campaign against the house? Nick was the only one with an obvious motive. He wanted me to sell up so he could get the money to move in with Ciara. I didn't trust Nick but at the same time didn't feel he would stoop so low as to do that. Then Cathy? Had she already fallen under Steve's spell at that stage, so he could get her to steal at will? At the time, I thought it might have been Sam looking for money for weed, and with the amount he was smoking, that was still a real possibility. I was left wondering if I had one person working against me, as in Steve, or were there multiple people involved? There were no easy answers, but I felt I had to move carefully before I came to any conclusions. Having seen what had happened to Fred, if there was some connection with what was happening to me, then I was in real danger, and not only me but my immediate family members as well. I was hoping Paul would come up with something for me to put my mind at some semblance of rest.

25

I finished work early the next day, hoping I could get a word with Paul. He tended to get drunker and more reclusive as the day wore on. I looked forward to having a bit of time in my own house when it was nice and quiet. However, when I opened the front door, I saw two mugs on the table but nobody in the kitchen. That made me think Nick might have been in, and he and Sam had done their slobbish lads thing by leaving the mess for someone else to clean up. That did cause a small surge of irritation, but I let it slide. Getting back early in the day was a bit of a treat, and I wasn't going to let that spoil it.

I put the mugs in the dishwasher and stuck the kettle on, turning the radio on at the same time. I liked daytime talk radio with its magazine-style programmes. It made you feel the world could still be a safe and welcoming place. Once I had my tea, I settled into an armchair to listen to someone talking about a good-value weekend break in the country. How I would have loved a break like that, more than a weekend, if possible, but just away from the estate and all the reminders of what I had been through. I was being soothed by the gentle, innocuous chat on the radio when I heard a noise on the stairs. It sounded like footsteps but kind of hurried.

Must be Sam, I thought and paid it no heed, but then I heard what sounded like a voice and a laugh. I had closed the door over so couldn't see from where I was into the hall, but the noises sounded unusual, so I decided to investigate. Walking slowly towards the door, I again distinctly heard someone whispering.

'Who's that?' I called out, and the sounds on the other side disappeared. Then I heard the front door open. I looked through the window to see the hunched form of Steve tiptoe out the door and hurry off towards his own house. The front door closed again, and I knew Cathy would be standing there in the hall. I braced myself and pulled the kitchen door open.

'What exactly are you doing?' I snarled.

Cathy looked dishevelled. She was wearing just a tracksuit bottom and T-shirt.

'Sorry, Mum. Steve wanted to see the house, and I had to get a couple more things.'

'I do not want that man in my house,' I enunciated as clearly as I could.

'Okay, okay, it's not such a big deal.' Cathy ran her fingers through her thick mop of curly hair.

'It is a very big deal to me. I don't let anybody in here unless I know them well, and I do not know him well at all. What I do know makes me worried.'

Cathy sighed. 'Mum, you're just down on him all the time because of his background. How is society ever going to move forward if people keep those same entrenched views?'

That sounded like a couple of lines from whatever text she was studying at the time, but I didn't let on. 'I make whatever decisions I like in regard to this house. He does not have a good history on this street, so until he proves otherwise, he is not welcome here.'

Cathy sighed again and marched off up the stairs. She reappeared a short while later with a couple of things and walked wordlessly out the door. I had to go sit in an armchair and catch my breath. I could feel my heart racing. A million thoughts flooded through me. *How long had they been in the house, and what had Steve been up to? Had Cathy left him to wander alone for any length of time? Had he been in my room? Was it the first time?* If he had been in before, it could have been him who took the money from my drawer. All sorts of possibilities ran through my mind, none of them good. He was the last person I would want to have in the house. Did he manipulate her to let him in? That was very possible. Did he know where she kept the key to the house? Probably. So he had access to my house pretty much whenever Cathy was out. He could even have made a copy of the key.

I thought about getting the locks changed, but then I would be locking Cathy out of the house unless I gave her a key, and if I gave her a key, I was back in the same predicament.

I was mulling all this over when there was a knock on the door. It startled me because I was in such a state of anxiety. I peered out the window before opening it and saw Paul standing there. He was an ally, at least, so I was happy to see him.

'Come on in,' I said, pulling the door open.

He walked unsteadily in to the kitchen table, where he sat heavily.

'Did you get anywhere with that?' I was suddenly self-conscious about speaking in specifics. What if Steve had bugged the place? No, but why would he do that? I felt like I was losing it completely.

'Yes, I did, as a matter of fact.' Paul was speaking slowly

and enunciating his words with exaggerated clarity as someone does when they don't want to appear drunk. 'I was able to make contact with some people who've been in the trade forever, and they gave me what they could find. Now, it's not much, but it's all they could get.'

'Not much is more than what I have at the moment.'

'Well, Brabazon Holdings was what they refer to as a shell company. It was set up for a specific purpose and folded straight after. Unfortunately for them, they never got as far as the specific purpose, which was to build the student accommodation behind your and Fred's houses.'

'Because we appealed it successfully, yes. But did you find out anything about the company or who was behind it?'

'Yes, I did, in fact. The company was in the name of a man called Peter McCann, who seemed to have very little history in the building trade.'

'Oh, McCann? That's interesting.'

'Yes, he had very little history, but there was no shortage of money there. He seemed to be ready to go if he got the all-clear on planning.'

'Anything else?'

Paul looked tired, like the effort of speaking clearly had worn him out. He eased himself off the chair and walked unsteadily to the door. 'No, I'm afraid that's it. You'll have to figure the rest out for yourself.'

That left me with a lot to figure out. I got straight onto my laptop and started googling Peter McCann, but the search brought me all over the world and onto lots of LinkedIn profiles but nowhere conclusive. Whatever Peter McCann had fronted the shell company that made the application had disappeared as quickly as he had appeared.

Of course, the one nagging question related to the surname. Chances were that Peter and Jim McCann were related and therefore in some way involved together. McCann said he had been in real estate and property all his working life, so it was quite likely he was involved in Brabazon Holdings. If he and Peter McCann were related, then Jim McCann was probably involved in the planning application to get the student accommodation block built right behind my house. During the planning process, it transpired that they would have knocked down Fred's and my house and put a road through there with the idea of transporting building materials. Without that, the whole project wasn't viable. Our houses were literally in the way of this huge development.

So how would I go about finding out to what extent Jim was involved? Despite all the outward charm, he was an elusive and secretive character. He never revealed very much about himself. Everything was allusions to this or that, but when it came to it, there wasn't very much I knew about his past. I decided I would have to get going and use whatever resources I could to reveal the real Jim McCann. He definitely had some sort of interest in Fred's house; otherwise why would he have mentioned the photographs? He had at least been snooping around, and I needed to find out why.

He had mentioned being away before, and he had that year-round tan to prove it. His look wasn't a weather-beaten one but one that had seen the softer side of the outdoors. McCann might have spent time on building sites at some point, but I could see him much more as the polished salesman of holiday apartments or something in that line. His voice was soothing and seductive as well, more the well-oiled salesman than the builder. Thinking back on my conversation with him, I remembered him saying he had been in property for the longest time. The way he had used the word had given me no real clue as to exactly what he had been doing. I spent a bit of time doing Google searches on Jim McCann and property. I did a whirlwind tour of Europe with my searches. First Spain, that being the most obvious, then Portugal, Italy and from there to the former Eastern bloc countries like Croatia and Bulgaria, which had seen an explosion of apartment sales, but I turned up no information on him. Maybe he had been somewhere more far-flung like South Africa, but I was getting tired, so I decided heading to bed was the best option. I ran a long bath and managed to relax in the steamy lavender-scented water.

As I went to bed, I thought about the encounter with Cathy and Steve earlier. I was going to have to have strong words with Cathy. She wasn't acting out of badness, of that much I was sure, but she was, as I saw it, acting out of naivety, and that was something that could be exploited, particularly by somebody with a history like Steve's.

26

I hadn't got anywhere with my Peter McCann search, so I had to figure the best way to approach it. If he was anything to do with Jim McCann, then the likelihood was that Jim would just outright deny it if I asked him directly. If not, he would surely have said something about it earlier. We had quite a chat the night he was in the house, and he hadn't mentioned anything. So either he was deliberately keeping quiet about it, or he had nothing to do with it. I decided that I would make very discreet enquiries and see if I could find out anything more about Jim's background. That might yield some valuable clues. Doing a bit of gardening later on might just give me the opportunity to snare McCann when he was making one of his frequent visits to Philly, his nephew.

With that in mind, I got out the pruning shears after dinner and started doing a bit of snipping. I also had my little trowel and a bag of peat moss, so I was able to freshen up the flowerbeds. I was working away at that when I heard a bit of noise coming from Steve's house. It was the sound of people chatting at high volume, so I turned discreetly in that direction to catch a glimpse of what was going on.

To my surprise, shock even, I saw that Steve was standing on the steps of his house with none other than the couple who had made the offer on my house and then subsequently gone on to buy Fred's place. Looking at them, I could see they were having quite a relaxed and jovial banter before Steve slapped Eamon heartily on the back, and they all parted company. Stephanie and Eamon hopped into a car outside Steve's drive and took off.

A number of thoughts went through my head as I watched them drive away. They had just bought the house, so maybe somehow, they had got to know Steve in the process, but the interaction I had just witnessed seemed way too familiar for people who had recently met. The other option, I supposed, was that they knew Steve from the car trade, and he had been fixing their car. That was a more plausible explanation, but still, it all seemed a bit too matey for that. So then, what? Were they involved with him in some nefarious deal? I was pretty sure Steve hadn't turned his back on criminality the way Cathy insisted he had. He had a string of convictions that went up to quite recently, so to me, he had all the hallmarks of a career criminal. Instinctively, I had thought Stephanie and Eamon had seemed dodgy from the outset, so what was their connection to him?

I got a chance to enquire later that evening. Cathy came home briefly in search of college notes. I made her a toasted cheese sandwich and a mug of tea, and she sat with me at the kitchen table.

'Everything okay?' I asked her.

'Yeah, why wouldn't it be?'

'Just asking,' I said with a smile. I wasn't going to let Cathy get on the defensive. Otherwise, I'd get nothing out of her. 'I want to make sure you're not missing the comforts of home too much.'

'No, Mam. I'm a big girl now.'

'I know you are, but I used to love going back to my own mother's house for a good Sunday roast, I can tell you. Nothing like getting the home cooking served up to you.'

Cathy smiled at that. She probably considered it lame and twee, but at least it brought her round to a more amenable frame of mind.

I left a good pause before dropping my next remark in as casual a tone as I could. 'I saw that couple who bought Fred's house around today. I think they're planning to rent the place.'

Cathy examined the side of her cheese toasty before taking a bite. 'Yeah, they're getting it ready at the moment.'

'Oh, so you have the inside track,' I said with a laugh.

'They're friends of Steve's,' Cathy said through a mouthful of toasty.

'Oh, that's interesting,' I replied.

'Why so?'

'Just, you know, they moved so quickly on the house after Fred died.'

Cathy stopped eating and stared at me. 'You think there's something dodgy about them, don't you? Is it just because they're friends of Steve's?'

'I don't know. They were around before Fred died, looking to buy either my house or Fred's, and now they have got Fred's house.'

Cathy put her toasty back on the plate. She was glaring at me now. 'You think they killed Fred?'

'That's not what I'm saying. It's just a strange series of events. I think even you'd agree with that.'

'I don't agree with any of that, Mam. As far as I can see,

there's no connection except that you are taking the opportunity to trash Steve's character, as usual.'

'That's not what this is about at all. Our neighbour was killed. There's been some very strange goings-on in our house that I haven't got to the bottom of. There is something going on, and I would love to know what it is. I am not in the habit of laying blame at anybody's door. That is a matter for the police, but Steve has a criminal past, and now he is friends with these two mysterious people. You must see why that's a concern for me.'

Cathy fiddled with some crumbs on her plate. Her head was down as she studied the crumbs. I could feel the tension hopping off her.

'Well, I have news for you, Mam,' she said eventually.

'Yes?'

'Yes. Me and Steve are going to start a family. In fact, we are already trying. How do you like that?'

I felt like someone had just kicked me hard in the stomach. The breath rushed out of me.

'Cathy.' I struggled to speak. Words weren't coming in any coherent way. 'You need to think long and hard before you make a decision like that.'

'I have, or should I say *we* have, because whether you like it or not, it's *we* now.'

I didn't like it, but I held back. How could I make Cathy see sense?

'Cathy, you are very young, and this is a new relationship. It is always advisable to approach such a commitment with caution.'

'So you say, but as Steve says, he isn't getting any younger. He doesn't want to be the oldest dad at the school gate.'

I could just hear Steve saying that to her with his characteristic cheeky grin slapped across his face. 'Steve already has two kids. That is a big commitment for him. Is he going to be able to manage a whole, fresh start on top?' I was desperate now. My arguments sounded old and hollow. I wanted to grab hold of her and tell her straight to her face that she was making the biggest mistake of her life. Not only was she making a mistake, but she was putting herself in serious danger.

'That's exactly what Steve wants is a fresh start. He does so much for those girls, but his ex just gives him grief over it.'

I could see Steve saying that as well. Blame the ex. As far as I could see, Cathy was in a pink cloud at the moment, and she would swallow anything Steve told her.

'Well, you only have one year of college to go. What's wrong with waiting a year? Nobody is much older after a year.'

Cathy ran her fingers through her hair. 'Nobody is much older after a year, but what if something else happens and then it's another year? Steve says you only live once, and he's right. Look at all these people around here who live like they're waiting for something to happen. We need to make it happen, Mum.'

'It's a mistake to rush into anything, Cathy. You know that, and this is one of those things you can't just reverse with a click of your fingers. It's for life.'

'I am able to think things through, you know. You need to stop treating me like a child. How am I supposed to grow up if you don't let me make my own decisions?'

'They are such big decisions.'

Cathy stood up suddenly and cleared her plate away. 'Well, as I said, they are decisions we have already made. The horse has bolted, or whatever that stupid expression is.'

Cathy got whatever she had come in for and left without saying anything else. She closed the door heavily after her to make sure I knew how annoyed she was. I was annoyed, but much more than that, I was worried, worried for her, but also worried for the rest of us. It felt like Steve had some master plan, and Cathy was just a small part of it. But if he got Cathy fully involved with him, as he seemed to be succeeding in, then I would become a hostage to whatever he decided to do. If I kicked back against him, then he could dangle the threat of doing something to Cathy. He would be able to use her as his trump card whenever he wanted. That was not a position I ever wanted to be in. But what could I do about it? I decided to give the detective who had given me his card a call. I could at least raise my suspicions about the couple with him.

I called early the next morning. He sounded tired, and his voice cracked, but he listened patiently. I told him about the couple and how they had seemed suspicious, and now I had seen them with Steve, the person who was causing trouble for all of us and the one Fred would be most likely to have a confrontation with.

'We've looked into them, June,' he replied succinctly when I finished. 'We are following up all leads related to the estate, and Fred's house in particular, so that couple have come to our attention. They have a little history, but all small stuff, nothing that would get the antennae up. Thanks for the call anyway, June, and if there's anything else, please let us know.'

27

I bumped into Jim McCann the following evening. I had decided to continue with my strategy of gardening in the hope he would turn up, and he did. He pulled up outside Philly's house, where, as usual, there was the sound of music coming from the front room. Sam was in there again. He spent most of his evenings in there after college. I did mind that he was smoking so much weed, but I didn't mind the proximity. At least I knew where he was, and whatever they got up to, it was a bunch of lads doing their thing. I did wonder about McCann being in and out so much, but Philly was his nephew, and McCann had properties he was looking after in the area, so it was no great surprise that he would drop by a bit. He also seemed to have so little family connection of his own that I guessed he appreciated whatever he had.

I waited till he came back out again, then deliberately made myself very visible. We locked eyes, and I waved over at him. He approached with that warm grin of the seasoned charmer that he had perfected.

'How are we, June? Those must be the best-tended plants in the city.'

'It's a pastime, and it gives me the chance to unwind.'

'Of course. You're in social work, aren't you? That must be very taxing but rewarding work.'

'Taxing, yes. You're fighting an uphill battle.'

'Business is the same, June. You're always working against the odds.'

'Was it always so for you?'

He shrugged. 'More or less. I wasn't born with a silver spoon, June. Life has taught me you have to fight for what you want.'

'Which is?'

McCann looked sharply at me as if that question had thrown him; then, as quickly, he relaxed again. The smile returned. 'What do any of us want, June? Security, a partner, a fulfilling life.'

He trotted out that list without any real conviction, like it was one he kept ready for use in his back pocket.

'Have you ever tried to go out on your own, you know, to get really into the business end of things?'

McCann did a little moue with his lips and then scrunched his features up as if the memory of such things brought a sour taste to his mouth. 'You know, June, I've certainly had ideas, but have I acted on them with any real conviction? I'm not sure.'

'I'll take that as a no, then,' I said with a smile.

'Oh, you could, June, you could. We all dream, though, that the big one is going to come along some day and put it all to rights.'

'I suppose. I have more modest dreams, though, that someone will be caught for killing Fred and that our street will return to something like what it was before.'

McCann's smile disappeared again. I could see him

visibly step back, like he was putting a physical distance between himself and the troubles on the street; then he nodded gravely. 'I know exactly what you mean, June. Things have really been turned upside down for you here.'

He looked serious, but his tone sounded forced, like he was going through the motions. He wasn't going to take any responsibility for the changes on the street. I knew I would get no further information from him, anyway. He was, as ever, keeping his cards very close to his chest.

'I'd better get back to the gardening. Not much light left now.'

'Yes, of course. You're quite right, June. Make hay while the sun shines, as they say.'

I was left no wiser after the interaction with McCann, except he seemed more on the defensive than before. Did he have something new to hide, or was he hiding something all along, just doing a better job of it before?

I tried to switch off when I sat down, but my mind kept racing over the different possibilities. I decided to distract myself by checking out some new reading material, as my current book was coming to an end. I fancied a bit of historical fiction, something I could really get my teeth into. I hadn't read any of the Wolf Hall books but had had them in the back of my mind forever. People had said they were hard to get into but were really addictive when you did, so I decided to take the plunge and order one.

I kept my credit card upstairs in a little wallet because I didn't really trust myself to have one at my disposal all the time. I'd run up a nice little interest bill a few years back that took forever to work off, so I preferred cash whenever possible.

I chose the book, put in my card number, and hit the purchase button, but the order didn't go through. Something was up, but I figured I was just tired so had probably missed a digit, so I tried again with the same result.

Strange, I thought, *I've hardly used it in the last while*. I tried frantically to remember if there was something I should have paid off earlier, but I couldn't come up with anything, so I checked the number on the back of the card and gave the company a call.

They listened to my story, checked the number of the card, and told me I was indeed overdrawn. They told me, however, that it had been used from my IP address. So whoever had used it did it from inside the house. They cancelled the card and said to call them again, and they would be able to give me some information on what had been purchased.

When I hung up the phone, I was shell-shocked. Whoever had done it had been into my room and must have had some idea of where the card was kept. Or else, I thought, it was somebody who was told where the card would be kept. After the recent encounter with Steve inside my house, I wondered would Cathy be that naive that she would tell Steve where to find it? Had he manipulated her to that extent? I found that scenario hard to believe.

As I was thinking through all of that, I heard the door close downstairs, and someone went into the kitchen. My heart started racing with real fear, and then that fear turned to anger. Why should I feel frightened in my own house? Even so, I approached the top of the stairs with caution.

'Who's that?' I called down.

I could hear the fridge door being opened and shut, and that actually put me at ease. They were familiar sounds and not the behaviour of an intruder, so I walked downstairs and into the kitchen to see Sam there, fixing a sandwich at the counter, ear pods in, shaking his head to whatever was on. I felt a final surge of relief that there was no threat, but at the same time, I steeled myself. I was going to have to ask everyone about the card, starting with Sam.

I fixed myself a cup of cocoa. I'd had my quota of caffeine for the day so needed something that wouldn't increase my jangled nerves. Sam nodded in my direction but kept the ear pods in. I could see he was preparing to bring his sandwich upstairs, so I indicated to him that he should take the ear pods out.

'Yeah?' he enquired when he had.

'There's something I need to talk to you about,' I said with a leaden feeling in my stomach.

'What?'

Sam looked a little bleary-eyed. My guess was he had been over in Philly's, having a smoke. Still, now wasn't the time to confront him about that.

'It's kind of awkward to even say it, but remember I told you that money had gone missing from my drawer? Well, that money never turned up.' Sam was frowning already, but I kept going. 'Now, it turns out that someone had used my credit card without asking me. It's overdrawn, and it was done from the IP address here.'

Sam's frown had increased, so it turned his whole face into a mass of creases. 'Yeah, and? You don't seriously think I used your credit card, do you?'

'Sam, I have to talk to everyone who has access to the house because it was used from in here. If someone had broken in, which I have no evidence they did, then they are not going to use the card from here.'

He was glaring at me from under his fringe of curls. 'I'm not a thief, Mam. You should know that.'

Even as he said the words, I felt a terrible pang of guilt flash through me. Here I was, sitting with my wonderful young son, accusing him of going into my room and stealing a credit card. But even as I thought that, I realized that he was also smoking a lot of weed, and any form of addiction can make people very deceptive. I had to broach that with him.

'Sam, I've noticed that since you've been spending time in Philly's, you seem to be affected quite a lot, which I guess is probably from smoking weed.'

Sam reacted by grabbing his sandwich and making for the kitchen door. He turned back towards me before he left. 'Oh, so you think I'm some sort of junkie and a thief. Well, that's nice, Mam. Thanks a lot.'

I was left sitting there with my cocoa. It felt like my whole life was unravelling. Everything was stacked against me, and I had to fight it alone. My own children were firmly in opposition to me, but I had to keep going. I had to find out who used the card and see if it brought me any closer to discovering who was waging this war against me and why.

I called the credit card company again and was left on hold forever while they retrieved my file and started looking through purchases. As I hadn't used the card for ages, it didn't take long for them to find a few purchases that had been made in recent weeks. When they told me the items that had been bought, I felt a cold chill of anger deep inside. They were all items bought in a huge hardware shop, and every one of them related to garden equipment of one type or another. I thanked them and hung up, knowing I need look no further for the culprit.

28

I tried calling Nick, but his phone was off, so I sent a text saying that I needed to talk to him next day if he didn't mind calling in after work. During that day, I tried as best I could to apply myself to my work, but my mind kept drifting back to Nick and what he had done. It was such a betrayal of trust after I had reluctantly given him access to the house.

I arrived home to find him sitting at the kitchen table, drinking tea. He was wearing his work overalls and looked tired.

'Well, what is it? Was there some news about Fred?'

I composed myself. This wasn't going to be easy, but then nothing with Nick had been easy over the last few years.

'No, actually, it relates to my credit card.' Even as I said the words 'my credit card', I saw how easily this had all happened. The credit card had been left in that spot for years with the understanding that we only used it for occasional online purchases. That had been the historical arrangement, so Nick was fully aware of where I kept it.

'Oh, something up with it?' Nick had an expression of

genuine concern plastered across his face, and I actually felt like hitting him. He was being so two-faced.

'Yes, there is something up, and I think you know quite well what it is.'

'Me?' He pointed at himself as if there could be another 'me' in the room.

I sighed loudly. 'Nick, don't come the innocent with me. It's getting very old.'

'Oh,' he said, slapping the table like he had suddenly remembered something. 'You must be talking about the gardening equipment that I bought for the business.'

I was astounded at the bald-faced nature of his act. 'That's right, Nick. Great that you suddenly remembered.'

'Yeah, of course, but I'll put all that back in, don't worry. I was going to say something about it, but I figured why get everyone all worked up when I was just going to put it back anyway? Better to tell you about it once I had done that. I knew you'd see it eventually on your statement, so I planned to have it back before then.' He was looking cheery now, like we had cleared up a little misunderstanding.

'Nick, you stole the money from my Visa card.' I let that statement hang in the air.

He shuffled in his chair but tried to keep the cheery demeanour. 'That's a bit strong, don't you think?'

'What I think is whether I should go to the police with this or not. That's what I think.'

Nick sat back in the chair and dropped his mouth open in surprise. 'You can't be serious.'

I picked up my phone and held it towards him. 'No? Give me a reason why I shouldn't.'

He shook his head vigorously. 'It's just the payment on McCann's end. There's a delay. I mean, he owes me a lot of money now, and it'll come through any day. I had to get some equipment so I could keep the whole thing going. It's not just for me, you know. It's for all of us.'

I looked straight at him. Little beads of sweat had started breaking out on his forehead. I almost felt sorry for him except I had seen his routine so many times before—the denial, the outrage and then the self-pity. 'Nick, you have never done anything for "all of us". You are a one-man band, and that's not going to change. It does surprise me, though, that you would stoop this low, to go into my room and take the credit card. And what about the cash?'

'The cash?' Again, he looked offended.

I nodded. He had taken the cash. There was no need to go down the road of excavating the truth out of him. We had danced that dance already.

'It was a loan,' he said with a croaky, almost tearful voice. 'That's all it was, a loan.'

'It was theft, Nick, and I accused your son of doing it.'

'You know, McCann was right.' The teary croak had left his voice and been replaced by a defiant tone.

'McCann?'

'Yes. He told me you're nothing but a ball-breaker. Now, I see he's right.'

'McCann? What does he know about me or our lives?'

'He knows enough. I see him a lot now, and he sees Sam over at Philly's house. It doesn't take much for him to put two and two together, does it?'

'What are you talking about?' I was genuinely baffled. The last name I expected in the middle of this was Jim McCann.

'He's had a lot of experience with women, and he knows when a woman is used to throwing her weight around. He says I shouldn't feel guilty about anything, that I was right to do what I did.'

I couldn't believe what I was hearing, but things took a

turn for the worse. Sam walked in and took a look at Nick, then at me. I saw him hesitate, like he was going to turn around and leave again, but Nick turned towards him.

'We're talking about the credit card and the money. I'm sorry you got accused. It was me took it on a loan basis, but your mother doesn't see it like that.'

'You took my money without asking. That is not a loan.' I was doing my best to stay calm for Sam's sake.

'I took it for gardening equipment because I'm waiting to get paid.'

Sam looked angrily at me. 'You're giving Dad a hard time again. He said it's a loan. Jim McCann is a good guy. He'll pay up, and then you'll get your stupid money back.'

I didn't know what to say. The two of them had taken a situation and turned it right on its head. I was the person in the wrong. But Sam wasn't finished yet.

'No wonder you and Dad split up if this is how you behave, accusing people of doing things they haven't done. Jim McCann is right when he says you've got a big chip on your shoulder and you just have to have everything your own way.'

I looked at the two of them staring at me from the other end of the table, and I felt a flood of tears rising fast. They were ganging up on me because of money that had been taken from me. I stood up quickly and hurried up the stairs to my room. I'd heard enough, and I didn't want to give Nick the satisfaction of seeing me cry, so I threw myself on the bed and sobbed into my pillow.

When I finally stopped crying, I lay there and tried to make sense of it all. The one name that kept coming up was Jim McCann. He seemed to have infiltrated every aspect of our lives, and now he was turning my own family against me. I felt like I was losing control. But why was McCann doing that? What was his end goal? He had probably been involved in Brabazon Holdings, which had put the application in for the student accommodation. Then he had seemed very interested in Fred's house, so was this some sort of fresh push to get the application for accommodation through? McCann had never mentioned anything about that, but of course, he gave very little away at all. I wondered if he was connected to the couple who had bought Fred's house. I had a strong sense that things were closing in around me, and McCann was somewhere at the centre of it all.

I decided I would have to find out more about McCann. I felt there must be some way of finding out about his past, and that would be the way to discovering what he was doing now. The pleasant, charming front that he put to the world was hiding something sinister.

Lying in bed, I heard the sound of voices downstairs, and I had no doubt that Nick and Sam were talking about me. I also had no doubt that what they were saying was probably negative and nasty. Nick would be playing the self-pity card to the fullest, and Sam would buy into it, partly because Nick put on such a good act, but also because of what McCann seemed to be saying to him over at Philly's.

It was then I decided. I'd had enough. I was going to sell up. Nick could go to hell. McCann could go to hell; the whole lot of them could go to hell. Maybe they were getting what they wanted, but I didn't care. I had reached a point of no return. I had to go.

Strangely calmed by that resolution, I went downstairs as soon as I heard the front door closing. I knew everyone was gone. Looking into the kitchen, it suddenly felt like someone else's place, like somewhere I was just stopping by. My attachment to the house had evaporated with the decision. The time for prevarication was over. I felt like a good, strong version of myself again. This would be a new beginning.

29

That sense of a new beginning was not to last very long. About nine hours, I think. I had gone to bed with my new sense of resolve and settled into a comfortable sleep. At some stage during the night, I registered the sound of the front door closing and knew that Sam must have come home. That made me turn over and slip back into a deep, warm sleep. The sleep was sharply interrupted at exactly six the next morning by a loud thumping on the door. It immediately brought me back to the bins being on fire. I stumbled blearily to Cathy's room to look out the window, half-expecting to see flames licking out of the bin outside. Instead I saw a small semicircle of police cars, one of them unmarked, like the detectives' one.

What can they want at this time of the morning? I wondered as I made my way down the stairs. I heard more thumping on the door, louder this time.

'Hey, take it easy,' I shouted. 'I'm coming.' I could see the outline of uniformed bodies through the glass at the side of the door. I couldn't understand why there would be so many. *Must be looking for information or have some new lead*, I thought.

Pulling the door open, I was shocked to see a policeman's badge flashed in my face. A plainclothes policeman was holding it, while those in uniform stood around him. They all looked very like they were about to barge into the house.

'Detective Desmond McGrath,' the plainclothes guy said, 'from the Drugs Squad. We have reason to believe there is a quantity of a controlled substance on the premises, and we have a warrant to search it.' Here he produced a sheet of paper that he waved in front of me. 'Now, if you don't mind, the officers and I are going to enter the premises and conduct the search.'

Shocked and unable to think of anything to say, I stood back and watched them flood into the house. There was one uniformed Garda with a dog straining at its leash in the background. He stayed where he was while the others rushed in. They split up into teams, some going into the kitchen while some went upstairs. I heard Sam's muffled voice coming from his room, as they must have gone straight in there. The noise and the chaos were hard to take in as they pulled out every drawer, lifted every chair, pulled out cleaning stuff from under the sink. One of them even started going through the bins. The motion continued until I heard a shout from upstairs, a lone male voice saying, 'I have it, boss.'

One of the uniformed Gardai came down holding Sam's puff jacket. As he held it aloft, he also held three small plastic bags with some off-white powder in them.

'Coke?' McGrath asked as the other Garda came down the stairs.

'Not sure, could be MDMA or ketamine. The lab'll clear that up. It was in the young lad's jacket.'

'Better bring him down, then,' McGrath said.

Another uniformed Garda brought Sam down. Sam was in boxer shorts and T-shirt. His eyes looked half-closed with sleep. McGrath led him into the kitchen, and he motioned for me to follow them in. Sitting Sam at the table, he put one of the bags with the powder in front of him.

He paused then and let Sam look at the plastic bag with the white powdery substance. 'Sam, would you like to tell us what's in the bag?' McGrath said quietly. I watched Sam carefully for his reaction, but he was just looking stony-faced at the bag. His colour was pallid in the early morning light.

'I don't know what it is,' he said eventually. The words tumbled almost inaudibly from his mouth, his lips barely opening to speak.

McGrath smiled at him and nodded at the package. 'Sam, it'll make things a lot easier for you if you just tell us. It's just me here and your mam. You don't want a whole palaver down at the station with every Tom, Dick and Harry asking you questions, do you?'

Sam didn't respond to that. He kept his eyes locked on the plastic package. I was willing him to say something and at the same time willing him not to. I was so shocked by the fact of the three of us sitting starkly in the kitchen, the police cars circled outside, that I didn't know what to think. All I knew was I wanted it over and I wanted him safe.

'I've never seen it before,' he said, again barely opening his lips. His whole body was stiff with tension, sitting poker straight in the kitchen chair.

McGrath shook his head. 'Sam, I want to make things easy for you. I can see you're a good young lad. You don't want to get yourself in any more trouble than you need to. We want this to be over as fast as we can. Nobody wants to see you in trouble, but it's best for you if you just tell me what it is, and we can proceed from there.'

'I told you. I don't know what it is. I've never seen it before.'

McGrath stood up and took the packet from the table. He placed it in a larger plastic bag and held it out from his body, like it was something contaminated; then he gestured to me to come to the hall.

'I'm afraid I'm going to have to formally charge Sam with possession of a controlled substance. If it is MDMA or cocaine, he has a couple of grammes there, and he has it divided into packs. That means he will also be charged with intent to supply. You can follow us to the station, and you are entitled to bring a solicitor with you. I'm sorry about this, but unfortunately, this is the way things have gone with young people now.'

With that, he led Sam out to one of the patrol cars. He was cuffed and put in the back. I saw his curly head hung low as the car took off.

I was left standing in the hall, trying to process what had just happened. I realized I had to act fast. Thinking about it could come later. I went online and scrolled through solicitors until I found one that had a twenty-four-hour service and called them.

Half an hour later, I was standing in the reception area of the police station, all bare walls except for little graffiti scrawls that let you know the nickname of everyone who had been there in the last while. There were some worn posters of dangerous dog breeds and some drug helpline numbers. The overall effect was bleak and intimidating. There were two thick double doors that led into the inner police station, and I presumed that was where Sam now was, probably still being questioned about the drugs. I stood there taking it all in, wondering how my life had come to this point. What had brought me here that I would be standing alone in a police station before most people had even got out of bed?

I didn't get time to ponder that question because a woman in her late twenties burst through the door a short time later and walked straight over to me. She had brown wavy hair, big-framed glasses and an officious air that I found immediately reassuring.

'June?' she asked. She proffered a hand for me to shake when I nodded. 'Catherine Horgan from Vine Solicitors.'

We sat on one of the benches that skirted the wall. Catherine sat in close to me and spoke quietly.

'I am here to get your son released. By what you said on the phone, the quantity of drugs is not large, so there should be no problem getting him released. They will charge him, but it's important that he doesn't sign a statement at this stage, so I'm going to go straight in. Is that okay?'

'Yes,' I said hurriedly. The idea of Sam being asked to sign a statement was very worrying. Sam was young and definitely not streetwise. He could easily buckle under any pressure. I knew the way the courts worked from my work, and having a signed statement without legal advice was bad news.

I had a very tense half-hour wait in the reception area before the double doors opened, and I saw a uniformed Garda usher Sam and Catherine out. Sam still had his head hung low. I was so angry with him but at the same time felt a surge of pity seeing him like that, so I stepped forward to hug him as he came out. We went out to the steps of the Garda station, and Catherine leaned in close to speak to me.

'Sam was released on his own bond. He is getting charged with possession with intent to supply, though. As I said, the quantities are not big, so we'll be contesting that. They'll set a court date, but we'll be meeting with you before that.'

I stepped into my car with those words ringing in my ears. *We'll be meeting you before that.* This was going to be a long, drawn-out, painful process we would have to go through. I felt sick in my stomach at the thought of it and didn't know what to say to Sam until we got home.

'Can you sit at the table with me? We need to talk,' I said succinctly as we went into the house.

Sam slouched in one of the chairs, head still hung low.

'Okay,' I said calmly, 'you need to tell me what's going on.'

'There's nothing going on. That wasn't mine. I don't know how it got there.'

'Sam, I need to get to work, so we need to sort this out. I have to know so I can figure out what to do next.'

Sam raised his head to look directly at me. 'Mam, I am telling the truth. I don't know how that got there. It's not mine. I swear. I'd tell you if it was because I know how much trouble I'm in. It's not mine, and I never saw it before. I don't know what it is. I swear.'

Sam was many things, but from the Sam I knew, he always had great difficulty in maintaining a lie. He never could from day one. Despite a few feeble attempts, he would inevitably buckle, so I was genuinely thrown by his insistence.

'But how could it have got there? Where were you last night, and how did the police know to come here?'

'I was at Philly's all night, and I don't know how they knew, and I don't know how it got there.'

'Who else was at Philly's?'

'There were lots of people in and out. All his housemates have their own friends, so there's always different people. Jim McCann was there for a while too.'

'Jim McCann?'

'Yeah, he's Philly's uncle.'

'I know. I know. Listen, why don't you go back to bed and get some rest? We'll get to the bottom of this, don't worry.'

30

That changed everything for me. If what Sam was telling me was true, and I was ninety-nine percent sure it was, then he was being set up, or rather *we* were being set up. It was yet another way to get at our family, to try to drive us from our house. Just the day before, I had decided I was going to sell up. Now, I had a very different view. If they wanted to fight, then I was not going to take it lying down. I was going to fight back and make them wish they hadn't taken me on. If Jim McCann was involved in this latest episode, and I was pretty sure he had some involvement in it, then I was going to get every piece of information I could on him to bring him down.

I got a break on solving the mystery of Peter McCann during lunch hour that day. I was scrolling through my own Facebook account when I did a search on him and came up with a load of profiles from all over the world. I narrowed the search down to Irish people and came up with quite a gallery of profiles, but significantly fewer than I had the first time. Some had just used emojis or funny images, but many of them used their own photo, and that was all I could search for. At this stage, I was looking for some particular facial characteristics, which I hoped had been generously shared in the gene pool. It took the guts of twenty minutes, but I finally found what I was looking for. I'm not sure if it was the boyish charm in the round face or the tousled fair hair, but when I saw the profile, I knew I'd found what I was looking for. There was no doubt in my mind as I stared at the picture in front of me that this man must be the brother of Jim McCann. There was also no doubt in my mind that this Peter McCann must have been the one who was listed as CEO of Brabazon Holdings. The coincidence was too great that Jim McCann would have a brother called Peter and that a Peter McCann had been involved in Brabazon Holdings.

I felt giddy currents of electricity flow through me as I stared at the profile picture. Finally, I had slotted a piece of the jigsaw in place. I wasn't sure where it got me in solving what had been happening in my estate or who was behind both the killing of Fred and the strange things that had happened to me, but I felt it was a step in the right direction.

However, the puzzle was made even more complex later that afternoon. I had an appointment in town, and when I finished it, I decided to do the rest of my work from home, so I landed up there about four p.m. I got myself a coffee and settled in to work at the kitchen table. The discovery with Peter McCann was playing on my mind. Now was surely the time to bring it up with Jim. I was pretty certain with my information. There was no way for him to wriggle out of it.

I was pondering that when I saw McCann pull up outside in his car. He sat there, probably doing paperwork, as he sometimes did. I contemplated going out to him but figured I would wait until he was actually out of the car. Despite the rage I felt towards him, it felt too confrontational to go over and knock on the car window. I had to keep my cool, to reel McCann in slowly. Besides, with all his false charm, McCann still made me nervous. I had seen how his mood could darken so suddenly.

I kept at my work, flicking an eye all the time to the car outside, and that was when I saw something that really caught my eye. As McCann sat there, I saw the figure of Steve come into the frame and tap on his window. McCann got out of the car, smiling, and the two of them settled in to what looked like a friendly chat.

That surprised me. If McCann had been onto Steve about the noise and the nuisance, as he said he had, then it would be surprising for the two of them to be so matey. Things took an even more unexpected turn when McCann opened the passenger door of his car and leaned in to come back out with an envelope, which he passed to Steve. They continued their friendly chat for another few minutes before Steve ambled back to his house.

I saw McCann go into Philly's then. I resolved there and then to go out and confront him with the information about Peter McCann once he re-emerged from Philly's. I grabbed some of my gardening equipment and went out front to snip and generally tidy up. As I was doing that, I had time to ponder what I had just seen. It looked like Steve and McCann were in some way involved together, and I wasn't sure how. Maybe it was just Steve as a tenant getting some documentation, but the way it was done made me think there was more to it. Usually, agent-tenant communication would be done officially through the post, but this was being done in person. The only reason I could think of something like that needing to be done in person was that there would be no official record. If it was something that had to be done unofficially, then what was it?

The beginning of an idea was starting to brew in my head. It was an idea that gave me cold shivers of fear, but it was one that I felt I might just have to do if I was to find out what was in the envelope. That idea was reinforced a few minutes later when Steve's front door sprang open, and he appeared with his two snarling dogs pulling at their chain leashes. He walked out tilted back with the strain of trying to contain the brutes and glanced over in my direction with that menacing grin of his.

'How's my future mother-in-law?' he said with a sneer before walking off up the road. I had noticed on days when I was at home that he took the brutes out for a long walk every day about four o'clock. It was that realization that had started me out on the plan I was hatching. Cathy had let slip a bit of information along the way—that they always kept a spare key under the mat so no one would ever get locked out. Armed with that information, I felt my plan could spring into action.

But first I had McCann to deal with. I felt myself tense up as I saw him walk slowly out the door of Philly's. He was taking his time, checking the house over as he came. He saw me as he neared his car and gave a wave over. I stopped what I was doing and walked to the low wall that bordered my garden, indicating I wanted further engagement. I saw him pause, his hand almost reaching for the door handle of his car. *Maybe he's had enough of me and my prying questions*, I thought. *Well, this time, I'm going to be a lot more direct.*

'Hi, Jim,' I called over, and he seemed to flinch at my cheery tone. He would certainly have heard about the drugs raid, even if he wasn't directly involved in the whole thing, but for the moment, I was going to say nothing about it. I would stick to the information that I was certain of.

'Hi, June, back in the garden, I see.' He still wasn't walking over towards me, maybe hoping our interaction could be short and cursory.

'Yeah, nature just keeps on doing its thing. Plant nature, that is. Human nature is probably no different, though. People have their own ways, and they keep on doing them, don't they?' McCann smiled, but it vanished as soon as it had appeared. I could see a flicker of impatience in his eyes. He was feeling uncomfortable, and that was exactly how I wanted him to feel, off balance, for when I threw the heavy stuff at him.

'You're being very philosophical today.'

'Or psychological. It's a fine line, isn't it?'

McCann scrunched up his face in a look of puzzlement.

'I wanted to ask you about something.'

'Oh, yeah?' He took a few steps nearer, so he was just on the other side of the wall.

'Yes, I'm sure you're familiar with the attempt to build a huge student accommodation block behind my house.' I nodded in the direction of the open fields that stretched behind my place.

'Oh, yes, the student accommodation.'

'Yes, the company that put the planning application in was one Brabazon Holdings.'

'Hmm,' he replied, still giving nothing away.

'It was a shell company set up by a gent called Peter McCann.'

McCann just nodded at this piece of information. I thought I could see his face drawing tight with tension.

'It was difficult to get any information on this Peter McCann, as he disappeared as soon as the company folded.'

McCann was just looking at me now. He'd stopped feigning any sign of neutral interest.

'I did eventually find his profile picture on Facebook, though. He looks just like you. Good-looking man as well. What's the age difference between you?'

'You think he's my brother?'

'Not think. Know.'

McCann looked at the top of the wall in front of him; then

he shook his head. 'You did a lot of snooping to find that out, didn't you?'

'I'm not sure snooping is the most flattering of terms for what I was doing. My neighbour has been killed, and I have been put under threat by I don't know who, so I am trying to find out what's going on.'

'That's fair enough, I suppose, but what makes you think Brabazon Holdings has any relation to any of that?'

'Maybe Fred found something out that he shouldn't have.' I couldn't resist coming out with it.

McCann's expression darkened, and he walked slowly towards the low wall. He kept coming until he was right up in front of me, within reaching distance across the wall. I found myself backing away unconsciously. His face had turned into a hard, stony version of the usual charming face he presented to the world, and his eyes had turned dark and cold.

'I sincerely hope you are not implying I had anything to do with Fred's murder. Words are dangerous. Very dangerous. They can harm people, but more than anything, they can harm the people who say them. You need to be very careful. Do you see any allies around you? Your son, your ex, your daughter? I don't think so. They have all turned against you, June. Your cries for help won't be heard. They think you are a liar. I think you are a liar, and you don't know when to stop. There are very dangerous people around you, but you aren't able to see it. You don't know who they are. For all your snooping, you haven't a clue.'

He stopped here to look me up and down like I was some sort of vile specimen that had just crawled out of a sewer.

'You don't know who they are, but they know you. Let me tell you this. They are watching you. They know your every move. Things can happen at any time. It could be an accident on the way to work. It could be in the dead of night in your own home. You never know, but all you know is it's not good to be alone, and you are alone. Maybe I am telling you this to help you. Maybe I'm not. You won't know, and when you find out, maybe it will be too late.'

I took another couple of steps back so there was good distance between us. He didn't move, and his dark gaze was unflinching. My instinct was to turn and run for the house, but I didn't want him to see my fear. I didn't want him to see me frightened and vulnerable because that was the effect he was trying to get.

'You are a coward and a bully.' The words just slipped out of my mouth. My mind was in overdrive. I was afraid of what I might say next, so I started backing slowly away.

'I am neither a coward nor a bully, but I do what I have to do to survive, and believe me, I always survive.'

He turned and walked quickly back to his car. I watched him take off at speed and disappear from sight, gunning his engine. I was so shaken by the encounter that I had to stand in my kitchen for a full five minutes, just looking up the road where he had disappeared with an angry roar of his engine. It was like I was expecting to see the car tear back down the road again and pull up outside my house. There had been a cold, detached sense about his anger that I felt was truly chilling. It was like a different person had stood in front of me, and they would stop at nothing to get what they wanted. What were all the implied threats? What did he mean that they were watching me all the time? Surely, that was just a figure of speech, but still, I had the sense that I was no longer safe anywhere, certainly not in my own home. How deeply was Steve involved with McCann? I had to find out, and there was only one way to do it.

I put the kettle on and made myself some chamomile tea to try to bring myself back to earth again. My heart was racing, and I could feel my hand shake as I poured the hot water. Sipping the tea at my table, I felt very alone in the world. I had outed McCann for something he wanted to keep secret. Nick, Sam and Cathy had all turned against me. Nick and Sam seemed to have been strongly influenced by McCann, which led me to wonder about just how deep his role was in all that was going on. Then there was Steve two doors down. He made no secret of his animosity towards me. He had Cathy exactly where he wanted her, and there was nothing I could do about it. I was the enemy now.

So what was the interaction with Steve and McCann about? It looked like they had some business together; otherwise why was McCann handing him an envelope like that? If there was something dodgy going on with McCann and Steve, then was Cathy being put in danger? She was way too naïve for my liking, and I could well see her getting into real trouble as a result of Steve. He was ruthless as far as I could see, and he'd get her to do whatever he wanted. Then the couple who bought Fred's house had been in Steve's as well. I had the feeling that I might just find something if I managed to get in there, so that was exactly what I resolved to do. I had to do it to find out what was going on, to protect myself and my family.

31

I hardly slept that night. My stomach was churning with acid despite the chamomile I had drunk. I'd spent the evening watching trash on TV, hoping to distract myself, but my thoughts kept wandering back to what I had to do. My resolve was strong, but at the same time, I was hoping for some revelation or some breakthrough that would mean I could call it off. No such breakthrough came. Cathy wasn't over during the evening. Sam was staying in after what had happened. He looked chastened and a bit scared, so I tried to pamper him with bits of foodie treats and generally gave him a bit of TLC.

'We'll take this thing one step at a time,' I had said. 'That woman from the solicitors is very good. Whatever happens, she'll get the best outcome for us.' Secretly, I was hoping I could get to the bottom of what had actually happened, but I wasn't saying that to Sam. There was an urgency to it as well that I hadn't mentioned to Sam. If and when the college found out about the drugs bust, then he would lose his scholarship and maybe even lose his place in college completely.

The next day, I finished with the appointments I had and

made it clear to my colleagues that I was available and online, but I would be working from home. My hands gripped tight on the steering wheel as I drove back. When I turned into the estate, it looked quiet, yet alien and forlorn. It had become a place of bad associations, bad memories. The street, the pavement, the hedges, all those things that had seemed to ooze a comforting permanence were tainted with menace. It felt like a place of sinister secrets, many of which were yet to be uncovered.

Steve was in his driveway as I pulled into mine. He was working away on a car, music blasting out. He didn't even glance in my direction as I stepped from the car.

I settled in as much as I could to do some work online. The kitchen clock was ticking, and I was fully aware of it moving towards four o'clock, the time when Steve usually took the dogs for a walk. There were some emails to catch up on, and I applied myself as best I could.

Glancing at the clock, I could see it was ten past four. The music was still blaring, so Steve was still working on the car. *Maybe he's too busy*, I thought. I hoped not, because whatever was in that envelope mightn't be in his house for too long. If I was going to make a move, today was the day to do it.

Then, about a quarter past four, the music suddenly stopped. I inhaled sharply and listened for any new sounds. Sure enough, I heard a gate squeak open and the desperate panting of his dogs as they strained at their leashes. Walking to my window, I watched as he was pulled by the two of them off and out of sight. He usually took them out for about an hour, so I had to move quickly. It was dead quiet on the estate, and I saw no sign of movement over at Steve's. Cathy was supposed to be in college, but I took the precaution of phoning her.

'Yeah?'

'Everything okay, dear? Just checking in with you.'

'Yeah, Mam, everything's fine. I'm in the college library, so I can't talk.'

'Okay, well, don't be a stranger.'

When I hung up, I grabbed the pencil torch from upstairs. It was bright, but I was going to search everywhere until I found the envelope. Looking up and down the street, I walked swiftly over to Steve's house. My heart was hammering in my chest, but I tried to keep my walk casual and relaxed. If anyone saw me, they might assume I was going to see Cathy. I walked as confidently as I could up to the front door and stood there a couple of seconds, turning to check behind me, but there was no sign of anyone coming or going in the street. Leaning down quickly, I flipped the corner of the mat up and snatched the key I saw there.

Turning it slowly, I pushed the door open and walked into the hall. Inside I got the smell of dogs, and even though I had seen them go out, I could feel a tremor of fear flash through me. The hall was messy with jackets over the bannisters and shoes thrown here and there. Old advertising flyers were left scattered where they had fallen inside the letterbox.

The layout of the house was the same as mine, so I walked quickly into the kitchen and scoured the counters and table but saw no sign of the envelope. I checked all over downstairs, in drawers and cupboards, but found nothing, so I had no choice but to go upstairs. With shaky legs I climbed the stairs, dreading being in the place where Steve and my daughter spent intimate time together but also dreading being in the claustrophobic confines of a very dangerous house. Once upstairs, I was trapped. If anyone came in, there was no way out. There were three bedrooms upstairs, just like my own place. I peered into one of them and saw twin beds with pink duvet covers and a couple of mobiles hanging from the ceiling. That was obviously the girls' room, so I turned quickly towards the other double room. Inside, I saw a wood-framed king-sized bed and a mess of clothes all over the floor. Cathy wasn't known for keeping a tidy room, and it looked like she had met her match in Steve. That made my job a little harder. I had to wade through the clothes to a big chest of drawers.

Moving gingerly over to the chest of drawers, I scoured a mess of small ornaments and jewellery on the top but saw no envelope. I had no choice but to start opening drawers, shining the pencil torch inside. Two of the drawers were filled with T-shirts and underpants, and in the corner of one of those I saw a vibrator, long, white and slick. I felt like slamming the drawer shut but kept on looking. I was there for a purpose, and I had to see it through. But I found nothing in any of the drawers.

Finally, I was faced with a built-in wardrobe. Opening it, I could see a jumbled array of men's jackets and shirts. The air inside it was dusty. I shone the torch around to see a couple of sports jackets towards the back, and I started to feel my way through the pockets of these. My hands were shaking as I patted them down. Time was running out. I'd been in the house a lot longer than I'd planned. If this didn't produce results, would I have time to search the last bedroom?

I was having no luck patting through the pockets of the sports jackets and was about to give up when my torch picked up a small zip-up bag on the floor of the wardrobe. I picked it up and unzipped it quickly. There, inside, I saw not just one envelope that matched the type McCann had passed over but two more of exactly the same type. I flicked one open, and inside I saw a small sheaf of cash. There was some sort of handwritten note in there too. I whipped it out and had a quick scan through it. It was written in a scrawl but said something like *Keep up the good work. I'll soon be able to put my troubles from down under behind me.* Just as I was struggling to read it, I heard an unmistakable sound that flashed a cold shiver of fear shooting through me. It was the unmistakable sound of Steve's voice outside, shouting something at his dogs.

Oh no, I thought, *he's come back early.* Glancing at the bedroom window, I saw specks of rain on the panes. It was raining. How stupid of me. I froze where I was standing, the bag still in my hand. I could feel my whole body go into a spasm of terror. He would be inside the house in a matter of seconds. Taking a deep breath, I slid the note back in the envelope and dropped the bag back where I had found it, closed the wardrobe door, and made a dash for the landing. I could hear the loud snuffling of the dogs outside. All I could think was that I'd have to tell him I was looking for Cathy. She had some medical condition, and I was worried about her. I knew he wouldn't buy it, but it might give me time to get out of the house and back to safety. My worst fear was that he'd come barging through the front door and let the dogs off the leash. They would smell me straight away, and God knows what they would do before he called them off. That was *if* he called them off.

I waited for the front door to swing open and be confronted by all three of them. There was literally nowhere to go. If I hid, the dogs would sniff me out, and there would be nothing I could say to him. But then, mercifully, I heard the side gate open. *Of course, he lets the dogs out by the side gate, so he'll put them in that way too.* The gate closed, and I knew he would be slipping the leashes off the dogs. There wasn't a second to waste. I had to take a chance and fast, so I dashed down the stairs, aware that I was making too much noise but hoping the sound of the dogs would cover it up. I opened the front door, slipped the key under the mat, and ran out to the right of the driveway, away from view of the side gate. The gate squeaked open again just as I reached the bottom of the drive. I saw Steve standing there, a look of puzzlement turning into that menacing grin of his.

'Did you come over to admire the cars?' he asked as I stood there.

'No, I was looking for Cathy. Is she in?' I could hear the tremor in my voice. That seemed to make Steve smile even more.

'Mummy's worried, is she? Poor little Cathy can't cope in the big, bad world.'

'If I want to see my daughter, that's my business.' I was getting over the initial fright.

'Your daughter's doing fine. In fact, we are doing fine. Never know when you'll get a bit of news. It won't be for lack of trying, anyway.'

He gave me a big, conspiratorial wink, which normally would have annoyed the hell out of me, but in the circumstances, I was very happy to let it go.

'Tell her I was looking for her when she gets back.'

'I will, that's if she gets time to go over, you know, between one thing and another.'

I left Steve grinning at his own foul humour and breathed a massive sigh of relief once I had my front door shut behind me. I had to steady myself against the door before I walked on into the kitchen and made myself a badly needed cup of tea. The hot liquid jolted me back into a clearer state of mind. I had narrowly escaped being caught by someone I had no doubt was very dangerous.

Sitting in an armchair, I thought over the find I had made. Steve had not just one, but a couple of envelopes that had been given him by McCann, and they contained cash. What was the relationship between them? Steve was probably well-connected in the world of crime. Did McCann owe him money for something, or was he paying him for something? Were they working on something together, and if so, what was it? Did it have a connection to the death of Fred and the various things that had happened in and around my house?

I would have to find out more about McCann somehow. I knew enough about Steve and his crimes. Did McCann have some darker history too that he had managed to cover up? I had to find out, and I wouldn't rest till I did. I was just about to go online and start searching for news items from all over the world with the name McCann in them when I remembered something that made my heart skip a beat—the pencil torch I had brought over. I had left it on the chest of drawers as I was looking in the envelopes, and that was when I had heard Steve coming back. I realized I'd left the torch there as I dashed onto the landing. Steve would see it. He might think it was Cathy's, but when he asked her about it, she would say she'd seen it in our house, but she had never brought it over. Would Steve put two and two together? He had seen me at the bottom of his drive, a place I had never been before. The torch had appeared mysteriously on his chest of drawers. Surely, he wouldn't think I would have the guts to get into his house while he was out. Or would he?

Just then, I heard a key turn in my door, and I felt myself paralysed with fear in the chair. Cathy appeared at the kitchen door and glared in at me. I was sure she had been asked about the torch, but no, that wasn't why she was there.

'Mam, do you have to check up on me, like, every couple of hours? Ringing me at college and then coming over to Steve's. You need to back off, Mam. I have made choices, and I am going to stick with them.' She disappeared as quickly as she had come.

32

I was left with a very uneasy feeling. No doubt, Steve was going to see the torch, and no doubt, he was going to comment on it to Cathy. She would say it came from our house and she couldn't remember bringing it over. Steve would think of me standing at the bottom of the drive, and he would really start to wonder. He had already shown how much animosity he had towards me and was, in my mind, probably the person behind the stuff that had already happened at my house. Now, what was he going to do to escalate the situation? He was not a man who liked to be crossed. That was quite apparent. But how far would he go if he felt someone had got into his house? He would figure out that Cathy had mentioned the key under the mat and that was a way for me to get in. The question was, would he think I had the courage to actually go into the lion's den, and what would I have been looking for if I had? He would know for sure that I had my suspicions of him and what he was up to.

At the same time, I had discovered the money there and was now more certain than ever that he was up to no good. After all that had gone on and with the death of Fred, I had no choice but to follow through and try to get to the bottom of the whole thing. I had reached a point where I couldn't turn back now. It was me against Steve and McCann and whoever else might be out there trying to do us harm. I really wasn't sure how many might be involved or what they were trying to achieve, but I knew I had to see it through.

I felt there was one way I could find out whether Steve had figured out that I had made my way into his house. It would mean I had to have a short conversation with Cathy later on. I would have to invent a pretext for that conversation, as she didn't seem like she wanted to talk to me at all now.

I had a busy day at work, as I had two clients to attend to and to find emergency accommodation for, so there was no time for further searching until I got home that evening. Before I was able to start, though, Cathy arrived in to get something. She breezed in and up the stairs without saying anything, and I was afraid she'd try to get out again without saying anything, so I stopped her in the hallway. I had already rehearsed my lines.

'Cathy, I know you'll think I'm being the overbearing mother again, but I thought I should warn you, there's been a couple of break-ins in the neighbourhood. I'm just conscious that you leave your key out.'

Cathy looked at me for a very long few seconds before replying. 'Funny you should say that, Mam. A torch that used to be lying around here turned up in our place, and I don't remember bringing it in. Anyway, Steve has decided to stop leaving the key there. Says it's too dodgy with the girls around the house.' With that, she breezed back out again.

I was left with a sinking feeling in my stomach. Steve obviously thought there was something up. He *had* put two and two together. I would have to move fast. I really didn't know what Steve might do next, and I didn't want to find out.

I could find something on McCann, even something that would bring me somewhere closer to piecing it all together.

I now felt I had a starting point. He had mentioned in the note that he would be able to put his troubles from down under behind him. That pointed clearly to something having happened in Australia. When I thought about it, that made sense. So many Irish people still went to Australia to try to make a life for themselves. It would be an obvious spot for McCann to go and try to make his fortune.

I searched through all the main papers from Sydney, Perth and Melbourne but turned nothing up. Then I checked out a few provincial titles and started running searches through them. That was when I struck gold. In one of the smaller Sydney-based papers, I finally found something on a Jim McCann, and best of all, there was a photo. He was coming out of court, hands in cuffs, trying unsuccessfully to hide his face. The shot was from about ten years back, but he was still completely recognizable as the man I knew. I read with trepidation through the article. I was glad that I had found something, but at the same time was dreading what I was about to uncover. That feeling of dread intensified as I read down through the article. Jim McCann was, indeed, a very unpleasant character.

The charges against him were for involuntary manslaughter, and the story went something like this—he had been working in real estate, letting properties, but in this case, he had owned the properties, bought cheap in one of the less reputable areas of the city. He had preyed on immigrant communities, exploiting their vulnerability and need to get accommodation, often without the necessary paperwork. It seemed Jim McCann was happy to accommodate them all, squeeze them in as tight as he could, and get paid in cash. He had been raking it in until disaster struck. There had been a fire in one of his houses, and two people had died. There had been no safety equipment, no fire exits, nothing. It was described in court as a death trap. He had got a seven-year sentence, and I guessed, might have served less with good behaviour. That meant he must have set himself up pretty quickly as soon as he got back in Ireland, but of course, he couldn't use his own name because if anyone did a proper background check, they would discover what I had just discovered.

So he had probably set himself up using his brother, Peter, as a front for the business. He had wanted desperately to get back in the game and make a quick killing. I guessed he had been cleaned out in Australia. The student accommodation block behind Fred's and my houses was obviously one of his main targets. It wasn't hard to see that if he succeeded in getting planning permission for that, he would make a fortune. Part of the trouble with all that scenario was how he might have got the money together for such a big project. He must have had funds to tap into from somewhere. That was where I wondered if Steve came into the frame. Steve had connections in the underworld. Maybe McCann had got involved with people Steve knew and either borrowed heavily from them or had the money available to him if he needed it. Either way, I figured, if that was the case, then he was under serious pressure to get that student accommodation built and start paying back money.

This was a very alarming twist to the situation. I had suspected for some time that McCann was not the person he pretended to be, but I never thought he would have such a criminal past. It made him into a much more desperate character. From his past, I could see how far he was prepared to go to get what he wanted. Then the payment to Steve. Was he using him to do his dirty work? Had he even used Steve to kill Fred? I remembered what my neighbour Paul had said when I broached the topic of Fred's death with him. He had been quite emphatic that Steve had done it. But was it that simple? McCann could have connections way beyond what I knew.

I figured I was going to have to find some way to get McCann to give something away about his involvement in what was going on. He had said that I was 'snooping on him'. Well, he didn't realise to what extent and how successful I had been in my snooping, but how was I going to put the information to use without confronting him directly? He was probably a far more dangerous person than he let on and had played the game quite well so far. But there must be some way to make him slip up, I felt, and once he did, he might give me some information that I could bring to the police. He was almost certainly involved in what was going on in the estate. The only thing I didn't know was to what extent.

33

I got a chance to see McCann sooner than I expected and in circumstances I certainly wouldn't have expected. I had been mulling the whole thing over when I saw both him and Nick pull up outside Fred's house. This puzzled me. What was McCann doing there? The couple had bought that house and were going to rent it out. Then it struck me that McCann might have been taken on as the letting agent, as that was what he did. I watched the two of them stand outside and wondered if McCann was going to get Nick to do some gardening work, if he was indeed the letting agent. That kind of made sense. But it did make me wonder about the connection between Steve and the couple and then between Steve and McCann. I felt they must all be interlinked.

I waited a while and watched as they stood outside talking. They walked into the drive, so I wasn't able to see them any more from the angle of my front window, so I decided I would have to find some excuse to call across to Nick. I went out onto my porch and looked over, but to my surprise, they had disappeared into the house. I could see no reason Nick's services would be needed there unless there was something to do in the backyard. Fred had just a small backyard, the same as my own.

That led me to walk further down my own drive, looking across all the time to see if I could see them. The front door to Fred's house was open, but I couldn't see Nick or McCann. I stooped down to pick a couple of weeds from my flowerbed, and when I looked up again, the two of them had suddenly appeared in the door. I had to think of something fast, so I pointed towards a rosebush that was just inside Fred's property but was dangling some longer branches over the wall into my garden.

'If you're looking at gardening work, I reckon that rose-bush could do with a bit of trimming back,' I said, looking from one to the other.

Their reaction took me by surprise, as both of them smiled at me. McCann shook his head as he smiled.

'That's not what Nick is here about, is it, Nick?' He turned to Nick to give him a chance to explain.

'No, in fact, I am here as a prospective tenant. Ciara is coming over later to have a look. I just wanted to give it the once-over first, but it all seems to be in pretty good condition.'

'Eamon and Stephanie were looking for an easy tenant, and I could think of no one easier than Nick here.' McCann gestured with an open hand towards Nick.

'It's not like I don't know the area and the type of house, so it could work out really well.' Nick looked back at the house, nodding with approval.

I didn't know how to react. Nick had pulled a lot of selfish stunts in his time, but this looked like topping them all. He was seriously considering moving into the house where his neighbour had been killed, and not only that, but he was also moving in with the person he had betrayed me with, my ex-best friend.

'Do you think that's going to work out?' I asked.

Nick was still looking Fred's house over. 'Do I what?' he asked distractedly.

'Do you think it's going to work out?'

I could see McCann was looking at Nick. There seemed to be a faint smile playing on McCann's lips.

'Hmm? Work out how? As I said, I know the houses, so there won't be any huge surprises.'

'No, but moving in beside me with Ciara. Would you think that was a good idea?'

Nick shrugged. 'We all have to move on at some stage. We're grown-ups, aren't we?'

I checked McCann again. The smile was widening. I had to pull out every resource I had not to let fly at him. He knew exactly what the dynamic was, and he knew how selfish and egocentric Nick was.

'Maybe you should have spoken to me first before you decided we had all moved on, as you call it.'

'I didn't talk to you because I knew you'd just put up some argument against it. You're all right with your accommodation, so you don't have to worry. As I told you, we are getting kicked out of our place soon, so maybe I didn't have time to go down the road of asking permission before I put a roof over my head.'

I didn't want to give McCann the satisfaction of seeing us have a row in public, but I felt like I was going to snap. Nick started walking towards his pickup. He turned to me as he got near it.

'For what it's worth, I did run it by Sam and Cathy, and they were absolutely fine about it. That makes three out of four of us, which looks very like a majority decision to me. Now, I am going to collect Ciara.'

He jumped into the pickup and gunned the engine before

disappearing down the road. McCann looked at me and shrugged.

'I can see both sides of the story here, but he does need a roof over his head, and he could be a very handy tenant for Eamon and Steph.'

'I didn't think it's any of your business,' I hissed. He took a step back and frowned.

'Well, it is just business, June. You know, nothing personal.'

'Like the other stuff.'

His frown deepened. 'The other stuff?'

'We all have our past that we don't want resurrected, don't we?'

He looked directly at me, the warmth gone completely from his eyes the way I had seen it happen before, but he quickly turned that into a puzzled look. 'What do you mean?'

I wasn't going to get into it there and then about the fire, but I was happy to probe. He looked uncomfortable, and I wanted to keep him that way.

'Well, Nick and I have a difficult past that we don't want to reopen. I'm sure you have parts of your past you'd prefer not to revisit.' Again, the chill came into his eyes.

'You're probably right there, June, but the same could be said for any of us. There comes a time when we need to move on.'

'That depends on how we move on, doesn't it? If we do it by hurting other people, then maybe it's not okay, wouldn't you think?'

'Certainly, June. But some people's feelings get hurt too easily, isn't that true?'

Steve came out then and waved over at McCann before starting work on one of his cars. He turned the music on, shouting over, 'Hope you don't mind. It helps me concentrate.'

McCann took the opportunity to go back to his car without saying anything else to me. I felt alone and outnumbered. There was nothing else I could say to him there, but I knew I would have to be very careful. He had looked puzzled when I mentioned the past and things we all have there, but he had looked very cold also. I still didn't have the measure of Jim McCann, but I felt I had only scratched the surface.

I saw Nick return with Ciara about an hour later. I hadn't seen Ciara in years, and strangely, as we do for people we were once very close to, I felt a pang of affection toward her. That quickly disappeared when I saw Nick put his arm around her when he was introducing her to McCann. He had stuck around and got out of his car to greet them.

I felt there was nothing else I could say. Steve was out too. I could hear the music blaring. No way was I going out there, but I did have a question for Nick, so I called him later that evening.

'Yes?' His tone was abrupt. He was obviously still playing the victim card.

'There was something that was puzzling me with this whole rental thing, apart from the fact that it is deeply insensitive. The money. Has McCann finally come through with your payment?'

'Not as such.' Nick paused like he was thinking how to phrase the next bit. 'We are coming to an arrangement.' He put a heavy emphasis on the word *arrangement*. I almost laughed. It was like he and McCann were a couple.

'Oh, really, and what would that be?'

'He said we could have the place in lieu of payment.'

'So he's not paying you for your work? Are you going to be some sort of indentured slave?'

Nick sighed loudly down the phone. 'I knew you'd take a negative view of it. Typical.' He spat the word *typical*.

'It's not a negative view. I have a vested interest. You still owe me the money you stole.'

'Stole. That's a nice word. I told you it was just to tide me over.'

'Yeah, but now you're not getting paid, by the looks of it. McCann has you over a barrel.'

'I think we need to end this conversation. I happen to be in a precarious situation with my accommodation, and now I am being thrown a lifeline, and all you can do is pick holes in it.'

He hung up, and I was left staring at my phone. I should have known that I wouldn't get anywhere with Nick. He hadn't changed one iota. In fact, he had got worse. *Everything* was self-serving now. In the past, he at least tried to cover it up. I hadn't even bothered telling him about Sam and the drugs bust. That situation was bad enough without having Nick involved. The prospect of having him and Ciara living beside me was absolutely intolerable. As far as I could see, McCann was just stringing him along, but Nick would never concede that someone could just play him like that. McCann had Nick exactly where he wanted him, and he had me exactly where he wanted me too, by the looks of it. But what was his game, and where did he want it to end?

34

I got a call from Nick the next day, and for a fleeting second, I thought it might actually be of a conciliatory nature, but not at all.

'I've been thinking about the conversation we had last night and the negative tone you took to the good news me and Ciara got.'

'Yes?' I wasn't quite sure where he was going with this, but I got a strong sense it wasn't going to be good.

'Well, there may be a way for both of us to come out winners here. McCann says there are people actively looking for property in our street, and it might be a very opportune time to sell.'

'Oh, we've already discussed this.'

'We haven't discussed it in light of what McCann said. Maybe it's time for you to show a bit of flexibility.'

'I don't know what to say to that, Nick, apart from that I'm busy and I have work to do.'

'Oh, I should have known. Well, I think McCann is going to talk to you later, anyway. Maybe you'll listen to him if you don't listen to me.'

We ended the call there, and I could feel my blood pressure rising. All this incessant harassment was taking its toll on me. I wasn't sure how much more of it I could take. The day passed in a bit of a blur, and sure enough, when I got home, McCann's car was outside, and he stepped out to greet me.

'Well, June. Was Nick talking to you?'

'Yes, he was, and I'm not interested.'

McCann was looking at me without any hint of the boyish charm. I felt like prey in his eyes. There was a coldness there that I had seen glimpses of before, but this time, it was steady and controlled. The effect was chilling.

'Things have changed around here, June, haven't they? I suppose that's the nature of life on a street. It goes through cycles. Maybe one particular cycle here is coming to an end and another one beginning. Did that ever occur to you?'

'A lot of things have occurred to me in the last while, and not all of them are very nice.'

'You're speaking in riddles again, June. Maybe we should get straight to the point. Nick would have told you that I can get a buyer for your house, so maybe it's time you gave that serious consideration, for your sake, for Nick's sake and for your children's sake. Why go on suffering, June, when there is a solution? Maybe it's that Irish thing in us, is it? We feel there's something wrong if we're not suffering. Well, it's time to move beyond that.'

'I'm not interested in selling and certainly not interested in having any dealings with you or anyone associated with you.'

'That's harsh, June. I am just the go-between. Don't shoot the messenger.'

'I'm not sure what you are, but what I am sure of is that I don't welcome your involvement in any aspect of my life.' I turned around and started walking towards my front door.

'Think about it, June. You may come to regret it later.'

With those words hanging in my ears, I went into my house and closed the door behind me. When I sat down and had some hot food in front of me, I was finally able to give the conversation I had just had some proper consideration. It was the last line that stuck with me most. *You may come to regret it later*. Was that a direct threat? I now knew enough about McCann and his past to take those words seriously. So how far would he go to get what he wanted? That depended on how desperate he was. From what I had found out, he was probably quite desperate. He had done all that jail time in Australia, presumably arrived back in Ireland with nothing, and set himself up again, but how? He must have borrowed money, so then whom did he get the money from, and how much pressure were they putting on him to get the money back?

My thoughts were interrupted by the sound of a key turning in the door. I expected to see Sam coming in from college, but instead, it was Cathy. She stood in the doorway and looked in at me, then advanced slowly, almost coyly, to stand at the other end of the table.

'I've got some news.'

Usually, that would be a statement to make me curious and even excited about what was coming next, but not in this case. I felt a cold sense of dread creep through me.

'Or should I say Steve and I have got some news. Two bits of news, actually. I thought you should be the first to know.'

I wasn't sure what my facial expression was at that stage, but I remember trying my hardest to keep my sense of dread masked. Cathy didn't seem to notice either way. She was obviously buoyed up by her news as she shifted from foot to foot with the anticipation of telling me.

'The first bit is that Steve and I are going to get married.'

That was enough to drain whatever pretence of a mask I

had. My face must have dropped to the table because Cathy's giddy glow started fading fast. She stopped shifting from foot to foot and was staring straight at me.

'The other bit of news is that I'm pregnant.'

Whatever my facial expression had been after the marriage news, my face must have dropped to the floor after the second piece because Cathy was frowning at me.

'That is not what I would call a very happy reaction,' she said slowly.

'I don't know what to say.'

'Well, maybe it's better you say nothing, then. I was so happy when I found out. It's something that Steve wanted so much.'

'Cathy, have you thought all this through?' As I said that, I realized what a redundant statement it was. Whether she had thought it through or not, it was happening. I took a deep breath. Cathy was fidgeting with her hair. I could see the anger rising in her. How could I explain that this looked like the biggest mistake of her life to me?

'That's great, Mum. Glad to see you're so happy for us,' she said with a snarl of sarcasm.

'Cathy, I am happy for anything that makes you happy, as long as it is going to work out well for you. I just think you're so young.' Her youth was, of course, a concern, but it took a back seat compared to my concern over whom she was going to marry and have a child with, a known criminal who might have been involved in some serious incidents on our street, not least the murder of my neighbour.

'You're happy for anything that makes me happy? Don't make me laugh.'

She was just turning to go out the door when I heard a quick series of loud raps on the front door. Instinctively, I went to answer it, but as I walked into the hallway, I realized I should have stayed where I was. Steve was standing at the door, which Cathy had left open. He was grinning malevolently in at me.

'So you heard the good news?'

'She's not happy. Of course,' Cathy answered, having walked into the hall behind me.

'Oh dear. Is it the finances? I'll take care of that. I hear you're struggling—well, Nick is, anyway—so I guess that has a knock-on effect.' He kept the grin going, but his head was stock-still, facing me, waiting to see how I would react.

'No, it's not the money,' I said helplessly. For a second, I thought I was going to break down there and then, but I sucked in a deep breath and pulled my shoulders back. No way was I giving him the satisfaction.

'Well, it means security for Cathy, doesn't it? Now that she's expecting, I'm going to do the honourable thing. Security is important in this day and age, isn't it? You never know when things are going to take a turn for the worse. Cathy will be safe with me. Call me old-fashioned, but I think it's important to have a man by your side. Security, as I say. You can't have enough of it, can you?'

Cathy walked past me, and the two of them left, but not before Steve turned back to give me a wink with a mocking glint in his eye. I shut the door after them, went to the armchair in my living room, and held my head in my hands. The feeling of isolation I had the day before was back ten times stronger. It felt like the whole world was pitted against me. I felt warm tears ebb from my eyes and flow in a steady trickle down my cheeks. Once they started, they didn't stop. I didn't know how long I sat there, but they just kept on coming. I could feel my body drain of everything as they flowed like they were a part of me that was draining away. Finally, as night began to close in, I shook my head and took a deep breath. I had to pull out of it and fight. If I didn't, I would lose everything.

I thought back on what Steve had said. He had placed great emphasis on how important security was. I had no doubt that he was doing that on purpose. There were two possibilities there. Either he had figured out that it was probably me who had snuck into their house and was letting me know that he knew, or he was implying that now I was so isolated from everyone that my own security was very weak. I knew that already, but the question was, did I have more to fear, and if so, from whom?

That night, before going to bed, I checked all the windows and doors and made sure they were all locked.

This is no way to live, I thought as I lay in bed and tried to read. But what was I going to do? There seemed to be danger and hostility at every turn.

35

It was no way to live, so I decided I wasn't going to live like that. If I had to fight to keep the life that I had lived and enjoyed, then that was exactly what I would do. I wouldn't cower alone in my house. That was my resolve, and it was a resolve that was soon to be tested.

Cathy didn't drop by again the next day. She had obviously decided that I was someone who wasn't going to accept her 'good news', so she'd probably give me a wide berth. McCann was back around the neighbourhood. I could see his car outside Philly's. Sam hadn't been back to Philly's since the drugs bust. It was the one thing I had asked of him, and he was happy to comply. The whole thing had really put the wind up him. He had a soccer match outside the county that evening, though, so he was going to be late back. I spent the night alone, except for the company of Tammy, who seemed completely flaked out on the couch beside me. I left her there when I went up to bed. It took me a good hour to get showered, take the day's makeup off and rub some moisturizer in. I was looking pink-faced and fresh by the time I was ready for bed.

It was then I heard Tammy meow. The sound was coming from outside. I had left her fast asleep on the couch, and it seemed too sudden for her to be outside. She was a lazy cat, and it took her ages to get round to doing anything. I went to Cathy's window, which has a view out onto the street, and had a quick scour around to see if I could spot Tammy. I did see her, scuttling hurriedly under my car in the drive. She would sometimes go under the car just after I came home in the evening, but that was to soak up the remnants of heat from the engine. Running under the car at this hour seemed more like she was hiding or something had disturbed her.

Looking out, I could see there was light falling on the car. Our streetlights are dotted with big spaces in between along our street. The nearest one to me is outside Philly's house. That casts enough light at our end of the cul-de-sac, but it lights the back of my car, not the front, and I could clearly see the front part had light thrown on it. That light, which was steady, was not being produced by some handheld device. It was being produced by a light from my own house. I had left the hall light on, as I usually do. It helps when Sam is trying to put the key in the door and means there is less chance he'll wake me up. He knows the routine at this stage, so he turns it off when he comes in. The only conclusion I could come to was that the hall light was spilling out through my front door, which must be open.

Now, I did feel I was in a distracted state of mind with all that was going on, but the last thing I would do would be to leave the front door open. The only possibility I could come up with was that Sam had come in while I was in the shower and had somehow left the front door open. Maybe he had hurried in to go to the downstairs toilet. That scenario seemed unlikely, though.

There was nothing for it. I had to go and check. If it wasn't Sam, then who was it? Cathy? She didn't seem like she was going to make any contact with me, least of all come creeping in at eleven o'clock at night. I walked to the top of the stairs, my heart thumping in my chest. It was difficult to breathe. The fear that coursed through me was like ice. It numbed my limbs and made me feel floppy and weak. Briefly, I had a flash of inspiration where I thought of grabbing my phone and ringing both Sam and Cathy, but I realized my phone was sitting in my bag in the kitchen.

Before going down any steps, I waited and listened. Not a sound. Worse still, the kitchen light was off, just as I had left it. That meant Sam was definitely not there. If Cathy had come in, she would have put the light on and might have turned it off again.

'Hello, is there anyone there?' I called shakily down the stairs. No reply. No sound from downstairs. Then a movement at the door. I jumped back to press myself against the wall, but then I saw Tammy push a tentative tabby head around the front door and walk slowly into the hall. She seemed to be checking left and right as she came in. Did that mean there was still somebody downstairs? The door into the kitchen-cum-living room was partially closed. I usually leave that open when I go to bed so that Tammy has free rein to go in and out. It was possible I had unconsciously pulled it after me. But if I hadn't and there was somebody there, were they waiting behind the door? My instinct was to bolt down the stairs and out the door, but if there was somebody there, were they waiting for me to do exactly that, and then they would jump out and grab me?

'Hello,' I called again, louder this time. I felt like shouting so a neighbour might hear me, but something about the sound of my own voice echoing in the hall scared me. No response and no sound came from the other side of the door. 'Is there anyone there?' I inched down the stairs, terrified that

someone was going to burst through the double doors and
rush me.

Keep calm, I told myself, but my legs were quivering with
fear. Walking was becoming difficult. I held the bannister and
took a long, deep breath, then continued inching down. The
closer I got to the bottom, the more I felt I could make a dash
for the door without being grabbed. Stopping to listen, I
could just hear the sound of a car pulling out far up the road.
How I wished I could be in that car, safe from the terror of my
own house.

Finally, I got the courage to make another two steps
down and was now past the halfway point. The place from
which I could safely run was mere feet away. Two more steps
and I steeled myself, muscles so taut with tension that I
feared I would just tumble as soon as I started to run, but I
had no choice. I had to get out. The thoughts of what had
happened to Fred were running through my mind, and I was
trying to block them at the same time. It wasn't going to
happen to me. It couldn't, not end my life there in my own
hallway, to be battered to death like Fred. One more step, and
I lurched for the door, almost falling as I did, but I managed
to regain my balance enough so my stiff legs carried me to
the bottom of the stairs and out the open door to the chill
night air.

As soon as I reached the end of my drive, I stopped and
turned back towards the house, waiting for sudden movement, but none came. The door sat open with the hall light
spilling out, but there was still no sound from inside. I
checked both sides of my car, realizing that whoever it was
could actually be lying in wait outside, but they were clear. At
that point, I wasn't sure what to do. The one thing I knew was
that I wasn't going back in the house alone. Paul seemed like
the best bet if he wasn't too drunk. I was just about to walk
towards his house when I heard a voice from right beside me

that sent me jumping back so I banged against my garden wall.

'Everything all right?' It was Steve. He was alone and looking at me with that mocking grin of his.

'Someone went into my house. I think they might still be in there.'

Steve laughed. 'You sure you're not imagining things? I don't see any damage. All I see is an open door and a woman outside in her dressing gown.'

I looked down at myself and realized that I was in my dressing gown and slippers.

He gave me a jovial slap on the shoulder. 'Do you want me to go and check?' Without waiting for a reply, he jogged up the drive and into the house. He came back out a minute later.

'Checked the whole place and not a sinner in there.'

'But someone had opened the door and left it open.'

'You sure you weren't tucking into the Pinot Grigio, June?'

'I am completely sure. It doesn't matter. Thank you for looking.' Fear was being replaced by anger. I didn't like his tone and hated the way he kept the mocking grin fixed on me.

'No worries, June.' He started walking back towards his own house, but then he turned back towards me. 'By the way, June, you know what they say. Just because you're paranoid doesn't mean they're not out to get you.' He laughed heartily at that, turning to look back at me as he walked away.

I walked slowly back up my drive. The prospect of staying the night alone in my house terrified me. But I figured Sam would be back soon. I could give him a call and ask him to get back. He'd understand if I was spooked.

Gingerly, I went back inside, closing the door behind me. First thing I would do was get my bag with the phone and call Sam. The kitchen light was on when I went in, and I looked around quickly to check for myself that nobody was there. Satisfied there wasn't, I reached for my bag, which was slung over the back of a chair. As I reached, a small object on the kitchen table caught my eye. It was the pencil torch that I had left on Steve's chest of drawers. The hand that was reaching for the bag froze in mid-air. A chill of goosebumps crept over me.

I had to sit down to stop myself from collapsing. How did the torch get there? Who had been in the house? The answers all seemed obvious, but maybe not.

Okay, so Steve had seen me outside my house and come over. How was it that he was the first person there? The obvious answer was that he had been in the house and was expecting me to be outside. He had gone in, either used Cathy's key or got in some other way. I had two locks on the door. One was a Chubb lock with a big key, but the other was just a Yale lock, and I knew anecdotally that burglars can slip them open with a piece of hard plastic. I got up quickly and checked the sides of the lock. There was what looked like the faintest of scratches there, but they could have been there a long time and offered no proof.

I was thinking there might be a second scenario where someone else had broken into the house, Steve had seen me outside, and he had used the opportunity to slip the pencil torch back on the table when he said he was 'checking' the place. He might have known someone else was going to break in and been working in tandem with them. Yet another scenario was he had got Cathy to creep in and used the cover of checking the place to leave the torch.

The worst thing was that he had left the torch there, knowing that I couldn't go to the police because I had got into his house without permission. When I thought about it, it was almost like he had wanted me to break into his house so he could have that extra hold over me. Had he actually told Cathy to tell me that they left a key under the mat?

I didn't know where to turn, but I wasn't going to spend the night in the house alone, so I called Sam.

'Yeah?' He sounded tired.

'Will you be home soon? There's been an incident, and I feel nervous here on my own.'

'Incident?'

'Yes, someone was in our house. I don't know who it was.'

'Did you call the police?'

'No. Sam, it's complicated, but if you're home soon, it'd be great.'

'Just getting off the bus, Mam. I'll be home in about ten minutes.'

He appeared, looking tired and dirty, a few minutes later. 'Someone came in the house, and you didn't call the police?'

'It's a long story. Cathy has a key. I'm not sure if it was someone from there.'

'It might be Cathy?' Sam looked at me like I was completely mad, then shook his head. 'What are you on about, Mam?' He dived into the fridge to get some food. I went upstairs and threw myself on the bed. The feeling of isolation was overwhelming. I felt I couldn't go on like that anymore.

36

I had the locks changed on the front door the next day. It wouldn't be enough to take the key from Cathy. Steve might have made a copy of it. Besides, I still wasn't sure who had got into the house and when. It was all a jumbled mess in my mind, and all I felt all day were rushes of panic. I couldn't concentrate on anything. Work went by in a blur. All I could think was that someone was trying to scare me very badly and that it could be a build-up to someone actually killing me. That thought was the one that surfaced most during the day, and at times, I found it hard to breathe. In work, I avoided talking to anyone wherever possible because the look on my face, I felt, would give so much away. How could I even pretend that anything was near normal? At the same time, nobody seemed to be on my side. Everyone thought I was just exaggerating or just plain imagining things. It felt like the world had been turned against me, and now that I was perfectly vulnerable, that world could finish me off.

Even when the locks had been changed, I kept looking out my window. I had texted Cathy to tell her and had told

Sam. He had just looked at me the same way he had the night before—like I needed help. I told him I wasn't giving anyone a key until further notice, not even him, and he just shrugged and said, 'Okay, be like that.'

'We got training, so I'll be late again tonight,' he said, and he looked at me half-pityingly before leaving. But when he left, I had that sense of being totally alone, friendless, in danger. If someone had broken into or come into the house the night before, what had they planned for tonight? I tried to watch TV, but everything seemed meaningless. They were just bodies moving around a pixilated screen. They were so far removed from my reality. I could hear their voices, but it was like they were speaking a different language. Even when the news came on, I just found myself staring at the news-reader's mouth, trying to put the sounds together into words. I switched the TV off and stuck one of my Spotify playlists on. The music was low-key jazz and electronic, and in better times it would have soothed me, set my heart to a slower rhythm, but now it sounded like a soundtrack that was building up to some ultimate calamity. That reflected exactly how I felt. The tension was tying my stomach in knots. I wanted to scream or smash something, to find release in some way.

Then I saw the familiar form of McCann's Merc pulling up outside Fred's house. I watched him sit in the car for some minutes, looking down at his lap, probably scrolling through his phone. Looking at him caused two major reactions in me. The first was fear. What was he doing there? Who was he in contact with if he was on his phone? Was tonight the night I was going to be killed, and was he involved?

The second reaction was anger. Everything on our street had changed since McCann and Steve had arrived. Fred was dead and nobody caught for the crime yet. I lived in fear every day, not knowing what to expect next. Cathy was tangled up in a situation that was way out of her control and could lead to complete disaster. Sam was now in trouble with the law and in danger of losing his college place. Nick was moving closer and closer, bringing his own self-interest and selfishness with him. If he moved in next door with Ciara, then that was my life over. I would have to go. There was no way I could live beside them, see them day in, day out. That was if I lived to see those days at all.

Desperation hovered like a thick black cloud around me. I felt completely trapped in a world not of my making. There had to be a way out, no matter what. Nothing could be worse than this. I saw McCann step from his car and walk up Fred's drive. He didn't reappear, so I presumed he had gone into the house. I checked my breathing. It was coming fast and shallow. A cold sweat had broken out on my skin. The slow understanding of what I had to do was seeping into my consciousness. I was going to have to confront McCann, tell him all I knew about him, and try to force him to react in a way that would get him to say something to expose what was going on, maybe even to incriminate himself in the heat of the moment. Nobody else believed me. I was going to have to do this alone. There was one thing I could do to protect myself, though. I grabbed my phone and turned the microphone on to *Record*.

I took a deep breath before walking out my front door. The phone was in my jacket pocket. It sat there like a leaden weight. The knowledge that I was trying to entrap McCann made my legs go weak. This was a man I now thought capable of anything. I walked slowly up Fred's drive. My body was willing me to stop, to turn around and forget about it all, just to leave this place, but my mind was willing me on. I couldn't let this happen to my life, to my street. Someone had to fight back, and that someone was me.

The front door to Fred's was slightly open. I pushed

against it and called, 'Hello,' in a tremulous voice. The hallway was bare, and my shaking voice echoed off the walls. I could see work was being done, wallpaper stripped, and buckets of paint and some tools lay around the place.

I could hear a noise coming from upstairs. McCann sounded like he was in one of the bedrooms. I stepped in a little further and called, 'Hello,' again. The sounds from upstairs stopped. McCann appeared suddenly at the top of the stairs. The light behind him turned his fair hair white, and his tanned face contrasted with the white, so he looked like a photographic negative. The effect was otherworldly and chilling. I felt like turning and dashing out the door, but I had come too far.

'Yes, June?' he asked in a cold, flat tone.

'I wanted to talk to you.'

'Again? We've talked quite a bit, and to be honest, I haven't liked much of what I've heard. Is there anything more to say?'

'There are some things we haven't talked about yet. Things to do with your past.'

'You've been very curious about my past, haven't you? I am a private person, and I like to keep myself to myself. I'm sure you appreciate that.'

He was walking slowly down the stairs as he spoke. My instinct was to back out the door and get out of there, but I was determined to follow it through. I'd had enough of the life of fear and wondering what was coming next. If there was any way to stop that, I had to do it.

'I am curious, more than curious. Everything that happens, you seem to be at the centre of it, everything bad, that is. I want to know what your game is.'

He stopped on the stairs and smiled. 'You'd call it a game, would you? I don't think it's a game, June. It's a very serious matter. This is life, June, survival.'

'And that's something you're good at. All those years in the

Australian prison. They must have given you some great survival skills.'

He started walking towards me again, this time with a face that had darkened with anger. His steps were slow and measured, and his eyes never left mine.

'You have been doing a lot of digging, haven't you? Maybe too much. A man deserves to have a past, doesn't he? Don't we all have our pasts?'

'Not that type of past, we don't, and then it depends on what we bring into our present. What about Fred?'

That question stopped him in his tracks, but a slow, menacing smile started to twist his lips away from his teeth. 'Fred?' he asked almost casually. 'Well, he'd run his race already, hadn't he?'

'What do you mean by that?' But just as I asked that question, my phone rang. I froze. It was buzzing in my pocket. I couldn't think straight. Would I be able to answer it if it was recording?

'Are you not going to answer that, June?'

I thought he would grab it from me if I tried to answer it, and then he would see it was recording, but then I thought, if I could just shout down the phone, whoever it was would come to help me.

I reached in and fumbled for the phone. It spilled from my hand and onto the floor right in front of him. He picked it up and stared at the screen, then threw it aside so it smashed against the wall. In the same movement, he slammed the door behind me. I turned and ran into the kitchen. I could hear him racing after me. I ran around the kitchen table with McCann just behind me. I could hear his breath at my back. I thought of running for the front door, but he was right behind me, so he'd just slam it shut again. Having no choice, I turned and ran up the stairs. My only thought was to lock myself in the bathroom and scream for help. I knew the layout of the houses so well that I was able to turn on the landing and fling myself inside the bathroom, turning the lock in the door at the same time.

I could hear him panting outside. He gave the door a couple of thumps, then stopped to lean against it.

'You know, June, none of this need have happened if you and that old fool beside you hadn't objected. I needed money badly. There are certain people here who will give you money to get you out of a hole, but the interest, June, the interest. They don't tell you about that. This has to work. Fred was just like you. He knew too much about me, about Brabazon. We had a little argument. I never meant it to get so nasty, but I am a desperate man. I'm sorry, but you know too much too. You could get me in serious trouble. I am a survivor. I've been through enough, but maybe we can work something out. If you just open the door, we can talk. Yeah, I had Steve working for me. He was good but not good enough. He actually fell for your daughter, you know. Wonders will never cease.'

'You've done enough damage, McCann. You need to stop now before it gets a whole lot worse.' My voice was unsteady. I had opened the small bathroom window and was ready to scream out.

'I've done too much. That's the problem. I can't let you go now.'

'It's never too late. They'll go easy on you if you stop now.'

'They never go easy on you, June. That's what I learned in Australia. It's hell, and I never want to go back there.'

He went silent then. I could hear some shuffling outside. Then I heard a running noise, and the door shuddered as he banged against it. I saw the screws on the lock move with the force. Another couple of those and he'd be through.

'Help,' I screamed out the window, aware that we were at the back of the house and the nearest one was Steve's, but maybe, I thought, Paul will hear from the other side. *Crash.*

He had run at the door again. The screws wobbled some more. 'Help,' I yelled again. My throat felt constricted with fear, and my voice sounded high-pitched and weak.

I knew he was going to run at the door again. I could hear the shuffling sound as he backed away, preparing for his run. There was only one thing I could do. I opened the lock as quietly as I could and waited. Once I heard him start the run, I pulled the door open just in time to see him fly past me and clatter into the wash-hand basin behind. He slipped to the floor, and I took the chance to skip out and pull the door quickly behind me. I had the key in my hand to lock it from the outside, but my hand was so shaky I couldn't get it into the lock. Next thing, the door was wrenched open, and he was there, right in front of me.

I turned and ran down the stairs, but he was right behind me. I made it to the front door and pulled it open with just enough time to shout, 'Help,' again before he grabbed me from behind in a choke hold and pulled me to the ground.

'Now I have you,' I heard him say in a low growl. He started tightening his arm around my neck, and I couldn't breathe. I clawed at his arm, but he was too strong. The grip tightened more, so the last breath I had left my body. I could feel a rush of tingles, like pins and needles coursing through my body as it quickly got weaker and weaker. I knew I was seconds away from losing consciousness when a shaft of light fell into the hallway.

'Hey, what's going on here?' I heard a man's voice say and at the same time felt McCann being pulled away from me. I recognized the voice. It was Steve.

'What the hell are you doing?' he asked McCann. I turned, still faint and grasping at the place on my neck where McCann had me. He was standing now, facing Steve, who didn't seem to know what to do. It was then I saw McCann's hand inch down to floor level, where he grabbed a hammer that was leaning against the stairs and swung it full force at Steve's head. Steve buckled with a soft sigh and collapsed to the ground.

I had just enough energy to stand now and started backing off. McCann swung at me with the hammer, and I ducked back enough so the blow smacked into the bannister. The hammer got tangled in the slats of the stairs and fell with a clatter to the ground. I was already stooped down, so I was able to grab it and swing it in a sharp arc to smack right into his kneecap. There was a loud crack, and McCann fell to the ground with a scream, clutching his knee.

'You've broken it, you bitch,' he roared, but I wasn't interested. I swung at him again, cracking his collarbone, then again against his ribs and again, until I looked up and saw Cathy standing in the doorway, her hand on her mouth. McCann was groaning and rolling on the floor. Steve was groaning too, but he was starting to sit up, rubbing at a gash on the side of his head. Blood covered his ear on that side, so his hand was bloody when he took it away.

'Oh, my God!' Cathy rushed towards him and cradled him as he sat up.

Steve lifted his head and looked over at McCann. 'I knew he was bad, but I didn't know he was *that* bad.'

'Phone,' I said to Cathy. I had one eye on McCann, but he was still rolling around on the floor, clutching his knee and his side. I called the police. Steve was looking at me as I did, and I thought for a second he might try to stop me, but he didn't.

37

McCann was arrested and kept in custody. Apparently, the Gardai had him as number one on their suspect list for the killing of Fred and were just waiting to complete their evidence before they made a move. That was slim consolation to me, who had nearly become his second victim. But at least now, he was behind bars and could do no harm.

Or could he? That was the sensation I was left with. Did he still have a hold over Steve? Would the nightmare continue? Sam, to give him his due, became super-protective of me once he heard what had happened. He wouldn't leave my side. I had to take two weeks' sick leave to recover, and he spent all the time doing assignments from home, going out with me on shopping trips, being home every night and staying up downstairs so I knew there was someone watching the house while I wrestled with my shattered nerves and tried to get some sleep. He put his own worries about the upcoming drugs trial aside. I stayed in touch with the solicitors, but they said it might take weeks before he got a court date. However, it never got that far.

We were sitting at the kitchen table one of the nights when he looked across at me.

'Mam, I'm really sorry for all the stuff that you went through and the way that I was with you.'

'That's okay,' I replied. 'We were all going through a very hard time. Let's not forget, our neighbour had been killed. That was a terrible shock to us. People react differently to shock.'

Sam shook his head. 'I know, Mam, but there was more than that to it. McCann was over at Philly's a lot.'

'And?'

'And he spent this time convincing me and Dad what a bad person you were.'

'Well, there's a big difference between you and Nick. He should have known better.'

I reached my hand across the table to cover his. It felt warm and comforting to me. He kept it where it was, and we just sat there like that for a minute.

'But it's kind of hard to tell you, but it was me put the bag of cement in the drain. That was, McCann put me up to it. He said you were deliberately making life hard for Dad by not selling the house. That's the only thing I did, though. I don't know what I was thinking. You were right, I was smoking too much weed.'

'That's okay, Sam. At least you are brave and honest enough to admit it. I really appreciate all that you are doing for me now.'

So it was he who did that, I thought. *Well, who did the rest?*

As I was pondering that later that night, there was a knock on the door. Sam opened it because he knew I would be nervous opening a door at night. I heard him say, 'What are you doing here?' and I feared the worst. Who could it be now?

A few seconds later, the gangly frame of the famous Philly

wandered through the kitchen door. I recognized him from various sightings on the street.

'Mam, it's Philly. He says he has something to tell us.'

Philly stood awkwardly at the top of the table. He was twisting his fingers in his hands like a schoolkid who has been caught doing something naughty.

'It's about my uncle Jim,' he said quietly. 'And the thing with the drugs. I heard about it. Sam's been a good mate of mine. My uncle was over a lot. The night before the raid, he was over, and he asked me which jacket was Sam's.' He looked sheepishly over at Sam. 'I didn't know what he was up to until I heard what happened. My mam is his sister, and she says she is going to get him to admit it.'

And that was that. McCann must have realized he had no allies in the world and couldn't afford to lose the sister. He confessed, and the charges against Sam were dropped. I had never seen Sam as happy when he got the news. He absolutely knuckled down then and got all assignments in, kept the scholarship, and even had a thing to say about the weed.

'I overdid it, Mam, way overdid it. I was so upset about everything going on, I think. I'm going to give it a good break now. Philly reckons he's doing the same.'

I was, of course, dreading the confrontation I would have to have with Steve and, by association, with Cathy. How involved had he been in everything that was going on? Was I going to be pressing charges against him even though he was supposedly my future son-in-law? I didn't have to wait too long for the answer. Steve had been in hospital for a couple of days after McCann's attack with his head wound. It was quite bad, and they were afraid for a time that he had bleeding on the brain. Cathy had been texting me with updates. I didn't like to see anybody suffer, but after what Steve had done to us, it was very hard to feel sympathy.

They arrived at the door a day after he got back out. Steve

looked a little sheepish for once in his life. The arrogant, menacing grin had disappeared completely, and now, the hard lines in his face looked softer. His head was completely bandaged on top and at the side. His skin was pale and drawn. He looked truly shaken.

I suppose a hammer blow on the head might just do that to you, I thought as they took seats around the kitchen table.

'Steve has something to tell you,' Cathy said before turning to Steve, just like they were business associates and this was a board meeting. Steve's bandage gave him a slightly Frankenstein-like appearance on top.

'June,' he began in a crackly voice, 'I'm sorry for all the crap that I have been putting you through. It was me with the bins and the snake and the car alarm. McCann had paid me to do it and to generally make a complete nuisance of myself to get you and Fred out of here so he could go ahead with his student accommodation.'

'Yes, I had kind of figured that. I had a fair idea of what he was up to at the end.'

'The thing with Fred was horrible. I didn't know he had done that, but I thought he might have been involved or had got someone else to do it,' Steve continued. 'He assured me it wasn't anything to do with him, but I was real wary of him from then. I needed the money, though, so I couldn't just back off. Now, well, everything is different. Me and Cathy are mad about each other, and it's going to stay that way. Things will settle down now, June. You'll see a different side of me.'

I wasn't sure what to say, so I said nothing, just nodded and then smiled over at Cathy to reassure her.

'I'm sorry too, Mam. I acted like a right cow some of the time. It was just, well, I was mad about Steve, and I thought you'd do everything in your power to stop me.'

You're not wrong there, I thought, but what was going on between them seemed really genuine.

'I understand. I can see you're mad about each other. Maybe I will enjoy being a granny,' I said with a smile to Steve.

The police did call into me and asked about Steve's involvement, but I played it down. He obviously had nothing to do with Fred's death and was just being paid to be a hooligan and a general nuisance. I wasn't going to press charges. I felt I had to give him and Cathy a chance. We had all been through so much, I couldn't bring myself to whip it all up again.

Steve did show he had turned a bit of a corner shortly after. Nick, who hadn't even bothered to come down to sympathise after all I had been through, got cut out of the deal on renting the house next door. Cathy told me that Steve had talked to his friends Eamon and Stephanie and warned them off Nick. Besides, Nick never actually got paid by McCann, so he was broke. He was going to have to start over, raise money, and get a new place. I sympathized with him for about a nanosecond before I felt an overwhelming flood of relief that he wouldn't be working or living in the area.

McCann got done for grievous bodily harm to Steve and for assault on me and for the murder of Fred. He wouldn't be getting out for a very long time.

The days after it had all died down, I went back to gardening with a vengeance. Never had the smell of jasmine been so sweet or the sight of honeybees drifting among the heather been so reassuring. The garden was truly bursting into life as the slow momentum of summer warmth began to build in earnest. I watched cars drift in and out of the estate and remarked to myself that I now had no fear of them. I wasn't watching out for McCann or Nick or Steve in one of his souped-up drag racers. It was just like the estate I had known through all the years, quiet, respectful, a place where you could unwind after a day's work.

Steve and Cathy started dropping in some evenings. I guessed Cathy felt pretty bad for the way she had been, but I didn't let on. What amused me, though, was the way Steve managed her as she tried to do normal stuff around the kitchen. He wouldn't have her lifting anything or carrying kettles or doing anything that could be perceived as strenuous in any way.

'I *can* do normal stuff,' she had said to him at one stage. 'You can wait till I'm nine months pregnant before you start all that carry-on.'

I still looked closely at Steve when he was moving around my kitchen, at the hardened lines around his eyes and his stocky, muscular body, brimming with power in every move, but the one I saw now was a flipside to the menace he had been. The power was being used in a protective manner.

Sam had taken to sitting in with me. We started going through old box sets. Neither of us had seen *The Sopranos* when it first came out, and that was definitely common ground. The outward normality of a lot of the characters' lives was relatable, but there was always that sense of underlying threat. I wondered as we watched it how much of what was going on did Sam relate to the happenings in our own little estate. I wondered how much of it *I* related to what had happened in our little estate. I just thanked God that it had finally come to an end.

The End

ABOUT THE AUTHOR

Kevin is a Guidance Counselor by day and a psychological thriller author during his off hours. He puts an original slant on some common experiences and creates engaging stories with a personal twist. Kevin lives in Dublin, Ireland with three great kids, a frenetic Westie, Alfie, and a wife who makes him laugh, which is really all he could ask for.

Want to connect with Kevin? He'd love to hear from you via email - kevinmflynch@gmail.com.

Did you enjoy The Perfect Home? Please consider leaving a review on Amazon to help other readers discover the book.

ALSO BY KEVIN LYNCH